NIXON

HUNTER SECURITY BOOK ONE

LAURA JOHN

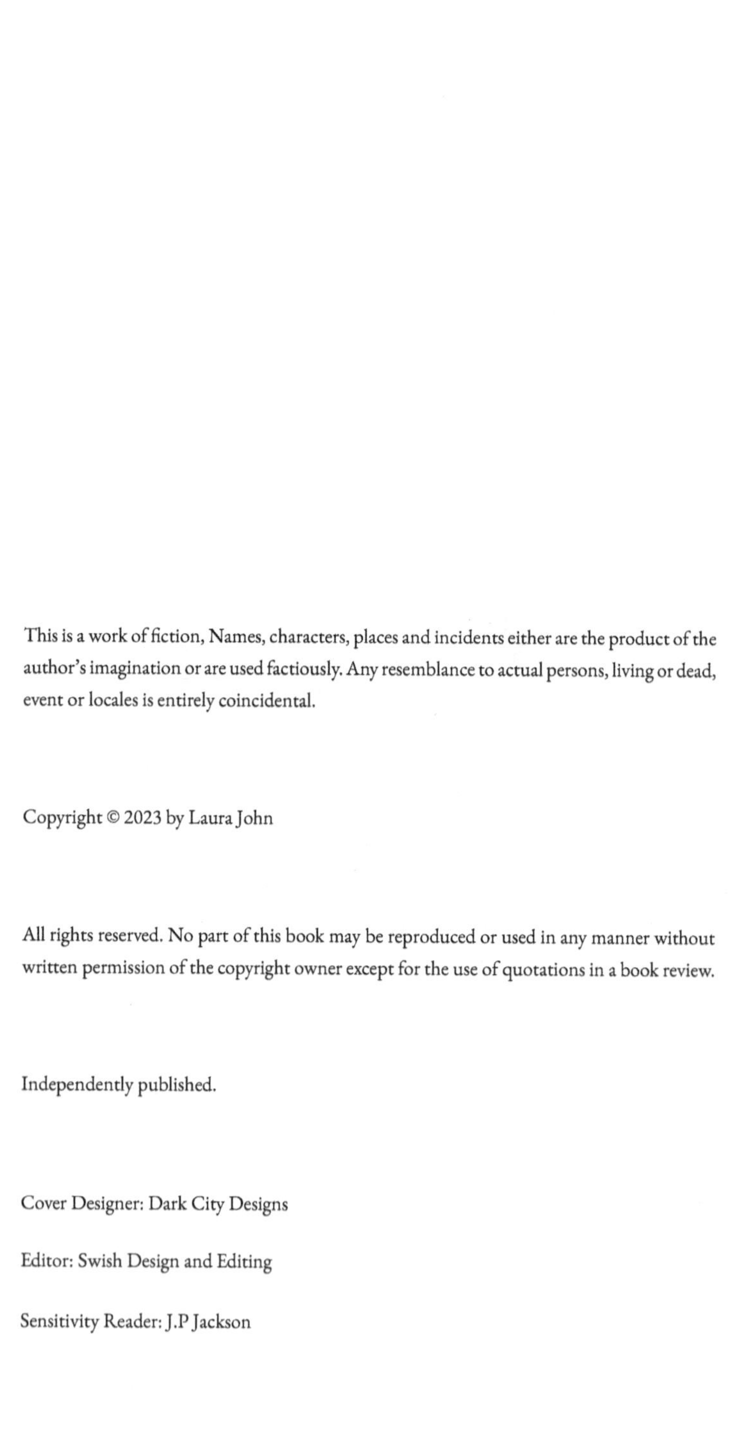

Dear Reader

This book touches on a few sensitive and heavy subjects that could be difficult for some to read.

If you think there is a subject that could be a problem for you, please proceed to my website for a complete list of content warnings.

https://www.authorlaurajohn.com/nixon

Chapter 1

Dante

"Dante, over here!"

Lights flash, and my skin crawls.

"Dante!"

Cameras click while I try to focus on my breathing.

"Smile, Dante!"

My head pounds, anxiety creeping its way through my veins.

"Grab Anna's waist!"

So much screaming.

"Kiss Anna!"

A pinch on my ass pulls me back into the moment of the red carpet, and I offer Anna a tight smile while she clings to my side.

"Don't let your anxiety get the best of you," she whispers with a giant grin on her plump red lips.

I don't know what I would do without Anna. She's the best thing that ever happened to me. She's my best friend, my person, until the day we die. The day we met, she told me we'd be in each other's lives forever, and it's easy to say that is holding true.

"Easier said than done," I mumble. "You know I hate these fucking events." Anna rolls her sky-blue eyes as she giggles at my whispered words.

"Maybe you shouldn't be the biggest actor in the world right now, then," she teases, and I laugh along with her.

"Dante! Anna! Over here," a scrawny man with shaggy brown hair and glasses yells at us.

I turn my attention to our publicist, Elanor, shooting her a questioning look.

"He's fine," she assures us. "He's going to play a game with you two. After that, you have one more interview, then it will be time to go in."

Anna nods, pulling us toward the guy.

"He looks out of place, doesn't he?" I murmur, but Anna shakes her head.

"You're only saying that because you haven't been paying attention at all tonight," she points out.

She isn't wrong. I would rather be anywhere but here. Hell, I'd even go swimming with sharks to get out of a red-carpet event. But as she stated, I'm one of the most sought-after actors in the world these days. Not only am I booked solid for the next five years, but I'm also a fucking household name. This is the life I always wanted, but the phrase "be careful what you wish for" rings true sometimes.

I was blessed to pick up an amazing acting gig when I was eighteen, much to my very religious parents' disapproval, and two years later, I landed my first significant role, shooting me into the limelight. Everything has been a sort of whirlwind since then. I know not everyone gets lucky like I have, and I'll forever be grateful for what happened in my career.

"It's so nice to meet you again," the dorky-looking guy says, pushing his too-big glasses up.

My eyebrows pull together as I cast a glance at Anna, who is giving me an I-have-no-idea-what-he's-talking-about look.

"Again?" I question with a tilt of my head, confused as I don't recognize him at all.

He nods with a big smile, showing off his yellowing teeth. *Seriously, who let this guy be on a red carpet?*

"We met a few years ago on the *Music in the Trees* set," he informs me.

"Oh, I'm sorry. I don't remember you." I say the words like I actually mean them. "There were a lot of people working on that movie," I add lamely, but it doesn't stop his face from falling.

Did he really think I would remember some random staff member from a movie I shot four years ago?

"So, what kind of game are we playing?" Anna pipes up, redirecting the conversation to where it's supposed to be.

"Right," he mutters with a curt nod. "I have a list of questions. I'm going to ask you one each. You either have to answer truthfully or take a shot," he instructs.

"Sounds easy enough." Anna beams at him, acting genuinely interested. "What's mine?"

"Have you ever fallen in love with someone you can't be with?" he questions.

My attention is on Anna when he reads the question, catching how her face falls for a moment before she corrects it like the pro she is. I know exactly who she's thinking about.

"We've all fallen for someone we shouldn't have at one point in time," she answers flawlessly.

"I guess it's my turn," I drone.

The man stares firmly into my eyes, ignoring the cue cards in his hand, forcing a shudder down my spine.

What the hell is up with this guy?

"When did you know you were gay?"

My blood runs cold. *Why would he ask that question?* I'm here with Anna, my girlfriend, at least as far as the public is concerned. But the way he's staring at me says he knows something he shouldn't.

"I promise you he's not gay," Anna answers.

I nod, forcing a smile so no one picks up on how much I'm panicking. "What Anna said," I add on. "I'm not gay."

Turning my attention to the beautiful blonde on my arm, I lean down to gently kiss her lips.

Anna giggles, using her thumb to wipe away the smudge of lipstick on my lips. She's stalling, playing the part, but I can't shake the uneasiness. "See, totally not gay."

The guy smiles, but it's almost unhinged. "Of course, I was joking. Thanks for being a great sport. Here, why don't we all take a shot, just for laughs," he suggests, handing Anna and me a drink.

We down them quickly before Elanor rushes us to the next interview.

"That was weird, wasn't it?" I whisper to Anna.

"We'll talk about it later," she assures me.

I nod as we are set in front of another interviewer.

I'm not sure how long the guy is talking, but his words suddenly sound fuzzy, and my head starts spinning.

"Are you okay?" Anna asks, her brows pulled together with concern.

I shake my head. My heart races and each breath becomes harder to take in. "I can't breathe," I tell her before collapsing to the ground.

People are yelling all around me, calling for medical attention, and Anna is promising me I'm going to be okay, but everything feels so far away.

Who knew I was going to die at twenty-four?

My eyelids flutter open to a bright room, and I immediately squeeze them shut. Then, as I cautiously try again, I'm met with a face full of blonde hair.

I try to speak but can't, so I lick my lips, but my mouth is dry, and it takes all I have for the slight movement. My entire body is heavier than it's ever been.

"Anna," I croak. My voice is rough, and my throat burns like I'm swallowing sandpaper.

When did I have a glass of water last?

"Shit, sorry." She sits up quickly. The pillow she was resting on falls into my lap. Fast hands run over her head as she tries to flatten her hair. "I'm so glad you're finally awake."

A beeping noise pulls my attention to a large machine beside me. It's then I realize we aren't home, having fallen asleep in one of our beds watching movies. No, we're in a hospital.

How the hell did I get here?

I scan Anna's face. She isn't wearing any makeup, and the bags under her eyes are dark. *Fuck.* Her lips are turned down, and by the tear stains on her face, it's obvious she's been crying.

Why is she so sad?

"Why am I in the hospital?" I question after studying her. My voice is still so raspy the words are barely audible.

She nibbles on her lower lip and reaches to hit a button on the wall.

"I'll let your doctor explain," she states and grabs a cup of water off the table beside me. Then she lifts the straw to my lips, and I take slow, small sips.

"You're not going to tell me anything?" I clarify before taking a few more sips. The cold liquid eases some of the discomfort in my throat.

"You were drugged," Anna whispers, and I gasp as memories of the red carpet come flooding back.

"Who the fuck drugged me?" I shout but grab my throat because it hurts like a son of a bitch. Anna brings the straw to my lips again, and I take a few big sips, trying to ease the burning sensation.

When a doctor, Elanor, and a beast of a man come walking in, my mouth goes dry, the water I drank doing nothing as I lock eyes with the stranger. *Holy shit, he's hot as fuck.* His striking baby blues pierce into my soul, and I feel like all the air has been pulled from my lungs. *Shit, I never react like this to anyone, let alone someone I've never met before.*

I've locked down my sexuality so much that this visceral reaction is throwing me for a loop. It has to be more than simply how sexy he is because I'm surrounded by people I'm attracted to all the time. Yet I can't put my finger on why my heart is racing right now.

"Are you okay?" a male asks, but it's not the sexy stranger staring at me.

If I break eye contact, is he going to disappear?

Is he a figment of my imagination?

"Dante," Anna calls out.

Forcing my eyes away from the man is hard, but I reluctantly turn my attention to my best friend.

"What?" I bark out, immediately hating the tone of my voice. "Sorry," I add on.

"The doctor is speaking to you. Where were you just now?" she questions.

I shake my head in response. We're surrounded by people who don't know my secret. I can't exactly tell her the truth right now.

The doctor tries again. "How are you feeling, Mr. Michaelson?"

"I'm okay," I answer. "When can I go home?"

"I'd like to keep you one more night to ensure your vitals stay stable. Especially with that random spike in your heart rate a moment ago. But if everything continues as it has been, you can go home tomorrow morning."

"So what exactly happened?" I ask no one in particular.

"You were brought in last night after collapsing on the red carpet. We ran several tests and found your toxicity report showed high levels of cocaine and fentanyl."

"Are you fucking kidding me?" I yell again, regretting that my temper is getting the best of me.

Anna is paying close attention and brings the water cup to my lips. I take a few sips as I try to wrap my head around this new information.

"Could this ruin my image?" I ask Elanor, who shakes her head.

I *never* use drugs. Hell, I barely even drink. But I don't want some fuckwad to ruin much more than he already has.

"We've made sure to leave out what was used in your attempted murder when we made a press release this morning," she assures me.

"If you weren't brought in when you were, you wouldn't be alive right now," the doctor states. His matter-of-fact tone causes my body to tense and my breath to catch.

"So, how long have I actually been out of it?" I question.

"Almost twenty-four hours," the doctor supplies. "That isn't abnormal, considering what your body has to do."

I nod, not sure what else to say.

"You're lucky you have such a great team," the doctor adds with a smile. "If you start to feel nauseous or dizzy, please let one of the nurses know."

"Thanks, Doc, I will." After he leaves the room, my attention is drawn to the sexy giant again.

What god did his mom fuck to get a jawline like that?

It's sharp enough to cut glass. And his cheekbones? Jesus, those are fucking masterpieces. If he isn't a model, he really should be. His beard could use some grooming, but that's a minor issue. My eyes travel down his body, even though they shouldn't, taking in his broad shoulders, thick arms, and delicious torso. He's wearing a shirt and a leather jacket, but I can tell he's got abs of steel hiding beneath it all. His tree-trunk thighs are encased in blue denim that clings to his perfect body.

I bet his ass looks amazing. Would it be wrong to ask him to turn around?

Shit! Of course, it would be wrong. I shouldn't be thinking any of these things. Instead, I should be demanding someone tell me what the hell he's doing in my room.

"Is anyone going to address the elephant... I mean, giant... in the room?" I finally murmur when no one offers up an explanation.

"I'm Nixon Hunter," he introduces himself with a low gravelly voice that goes straight to my cock. I'm extremely thankful for the pillow in my lap right now, preventing everyone from getting an eyeful of my erection.

Anna and Elanor might know my dirty little secret, but the sexy stranger sure as hell doesn't.

Nixon steps forward, extending his hand to me. I take it, and a zap of electricity shoots up my arm, making me gasp. With how Nixon's eyes go wide, I'm positive he felt it too.

Who the hell is this man?

And why am I reacting to him like this?

I pull my hand away, placing it on the pillow and tilting my head at him.

"So, Nixon, who are you?"

"Your bodyguard," he states.

I laugh. "Like fuck you are," I call his bluff, but when my eyes meet Elanor's, I stop. "Please tell me you did *not* hire me a bodyguard." I groan.

"Dante, you were drugged last night. What the hell do you want me to do? Let you walk around without protection while the person who did it is still out there?"

"I don't need a babysitter. Besides, the event last night had full security, yet this still happened. So what exactly will Bigfoot do to protect me that last night's team didn't do?"

"We didn't know you had someone out there who wanted you dead before," Elanor counters.

She's got a point, but I'm not going to admit that out loud.

"Who drugged me?"

"Our suspicions are it was the man you took the shot from," Nixon supplies.

"Wait. Are you okay?" I ask Anna, whipping my head around to her.

She nods, squeezing my hand gently.

"He must have only drugged yours," she guesses.

"But why me? If it *was* him, wouldn't it make sense to drug us both?"

"The timing lines up perfectly, and when I asked for the credentials of everyone working last night, I found out his were forged," Nixon informs me.

I shift my focus to Elanor, narrowing my eyes on her. "How *the fuck* does that happen?" My body heats with frustration. "You were the one who pushed us to do that interview," I point out before she can answer.

"I... I don't know," she whispers, stuttering as her bottom lip wobbles. She sucks in a breath. "I'm so sorry. I just trusted the officials and didn't think we had anything to worry about."

Something about her answer doesn't sit right with me, but it could be the anger clouding my judgment. I throw my head back and let out a deep sigh.

Why the hell does this have to be happening to me?

Yes, celebrities get stalkers all the time and people who want them dead, but I've been fighting off personal security for years. I don't want others all up in my business. I keep my circle tight for a reason.

"Dante, we knew it was only a matter of time before we had to add security," Anna states, trying to console me.

The only thing stopping me from fighting this harder is the fact that I don't want my best friend to get hurt. What if this person tries something else, and Anna gets in the way? I couldn't live if anything happened to her because of me.

"I have conditions to all of this," I declare.

"Name them. But I get veto rights over all of them. Your safety is more important than your ego," Nixon replies firmly.

I almost gasp. *Who the hell does he think he is? No one talks to me like that.* "If you think you're in charge here, you are sorely mistaken." I sneer. "You're my *employee*. If you don't step in line, I'll fire you and find a better security company."

"Good luck with that." He chuckles, raising a brow in challenge.

Now who's the one with the ego?

Not having enough brain power to fight anymore, I resort to scowling.

Anna giggles. "This is going to be so much fun."

I throw the pillow sitting in my lap at her.

Fun is the exact opposite of what is going to happen. I can tell that already.

Chapter 2
Nixon

DANTE GLARES AT ME as I get everyone's attention, ready to review a few things. Of course, his piercing eyes and the heated glare directed at me don't make him any less handsome, which is kind of irritating.

I'm extremely attracted to this man.

Ten years ago, I started Hunter Security when I got out of the Army, and for the first time, I'm wondering if I can be on this protection team without being distracted.

"The doctor is going to release you in the morning, so we need to go over the game plan for when you get out of here," I inform him, resulting in a deep scowl, which seems to be his go-to expression.

"Why does there need to be a game plan?" He scoffs, his hazel eyes shooting daggers at me. I bite my tongue to avoid berating him for his rude tone. "You can drive me and Anna home, then leave. I have a state-of-the-art security system, so we don't need you there."

"Stop being such an ass," Anna scolds him.

Brat is the term I would use to describe him, but ass works as well.

When he sticks his tongue out at her like a child while rolling his eyes, my hand twitches. *If he were mine, I'd tan his ass for that, but he isn't, and I need to stop that train of thought immediately.*

First, he's straight.

Second, he's taken.

Third, he's my fucking client.

"You're right about the security system. It's a good one. As of right now, you don't need a live-in bodyguard, but that could change if things escalate…" I pause, and again, he rolls his eyes. *Such a brat.* "I'm going to have another member of my team come along with us to escort you home tomorrow. Your house is surrounded by paparazzi, so the extra vehicle will make getting into your property easier. When we get to your place, I'll need to gain access to your security system. The system you have allows second-party apps to attach to it. That will let me get all the notifications. If, for any reason, you need to leave your house, you need to call me, and I'll escort you. Also, if you want any visitors, I need to approve them before they gain access to your property," I explain to Dante and Anna.

"This is bullshit," Dante barks out. "You do *not* get to tell me who I can and can't have over."

"Can we add people to the visitor list now?" Anna asks calmly before I can respond to Dante and tell him that I *do*, in fact, get to tell him that.

"Absolutely," I assure her. She smiles brightly in response, something I've yet to see Dante do.

"He's already signed the NDA, but remember, there may be listening ears around here," Elanor informs them.

"I'll make a list. We can go over it when we get home tomorrow," Anna says.

"That sounds perfect. What about you, Dante? Would you like to make a list of regular visitors?" I inquire, prepared for a snarky response.

Dante runs a hand through his silky brown hair that normally sits at his cheekbones and shakes his head.

"Nah, I don't like people," he grumbles.

"Well, that makes my life easier," I respond dryly. "Do either of you have any other questions?"

"Are you going to find the fuckwad who tried to kill me so I can go back to living a normal life again?" Dante growls.

The fact that he's doubting me makes me want to prove how good my company is. I've worked my ass off to make sure we are the best protection and security company out there. I put my all into the company, even going as far as to set up our head office where we are instead of my hometown. My parents hated me moving away but understood why I did it, and I've always been grateful to have an amazing support system.

"My team is working on it. I promise they are the best of the best. We'll catch him, but it's hard to say if your life will ever go back to normal. You aren't a nobody anymore. Having a permanent security team for when you do events or travel is probably a smart idea."

"You just want to keep making big money," he mumbles.

I desperately want to respond but keep my mouth shut. I hate asshole clients. Unfortunately, even dicks need protection. Sometimes more than nice people.

Pulling out my phone, I text one of my best guys, Denver, to take my place guarding the room while I head out to run a few errands.

"Denver is going to be watching your room for a few hours. I'll be back later," I state, stand, and head toward the door.

"Thanks for all your help." Anna beams at me, and I'm thankful she is going to be a part of this job. At least she'll make things a bit brighter.

"It's what I do." I shrug.

"I'm sorry Dante is being so hardheaded," Elanor apologizes when we are in the hall.

"You warned me ahead of time," I remind her. "He isn't the first person to think they are above needing security, and he won't be the last."

"He's a secretive person. He doesn't like having people in his life, and he doesn't trust easily. I've known him and Anna since high school, and I'm sure that's the only reason he hired me as his publicist slash manager. He knew I wouldn't blab his secrets to the world."

"They are high school sweethearts, right?" I inquire, making sure the facts I pulled up after background checks and a shit ton of internet sleuthing are correct.

Her eyes dart back and forth, and she presses her lips together before cooling her expression and plastering on a fake smile. "Yup," she responds, popping the *p*.

She isn't telling the whole truth, but I don't need to push it right now. I make a mental note to look into her further to see if I can find what she's not telling me.

Denver arrives, greeting me with a bro hug and a slap on the back. "No one gets in this room except the people who are currently in it, Elanor here, Dr. Murray, and that nurse right there." I point at a pretty young nurse.

"Got it," he replies and leans against the door.

"He signed the NDA already, right?" Elanor checks.

"Yup. I had everyone at my company sign them just in case," I assure her.

She smiles, appearing relieved. "Thank you so much for all of this. I know Dante is a lot, but deep down, he is a great guy."

I have no idea how to respond to that, so I don't. My impression of him is that he's a douche, but I don't know him well yet, so I'll try to give him the benefit of the doubt for the time being.

"Are you sticking around?" I ask Elanor, and she shakes her head.

"No. I'm just going to say goodbye, then I'll be heading home. I'll be back first thing in the morning."

"Perfect. I will see you then," I say and walk away.

I need to get my shit together, both physically and emotionally. I will not let the sexy brat lying in a hospital bed get under my skin. I'll do my job like I always do. And I sure as shit won't let a man I just met be my downfall.

Chapter 3

Dante

THIS MORNING, I WAS discharged with strict orders to stay hydrated and rest for the remainder of the week. After that, I'll be able to return to the set and get on with my life. Unfortunately, I will now have a new permanent shadow anytime I leave the house—a giant sexy shadow who has eyes that suck me in while he stares directly into my soul.

I wonder what he sees there?

Shit.

I need to stop thinking about him like that. The *last* thing I will be doing is falling for my bodyguard. I'll appreciate his god-like looks, but that is as far as I will let it go.

"I think I'm going to quit acting," I whisper to Anna as Nixon drives us home.

"You can't quit for at least five years. Contracts, baby," she teases. I glare at her, but it only makes her grin grow. "Besides, you *love* acting. You're not going to stop just because we're finally forcing you to have protection."

"Stop being right. Smugness isn't becoming of you," I grumble, and Anna laughs.

The rest of the drive is quiet. Nixon is focused like a hawk, not saying a single word to us. His large hands grip the steering wheel firmly, and the way his sleeves are rolled up shows off his thick forearms in the most delicious way.

Why am I getting turned on by watching him drive?

Ringing throughout the car jolts me out of my daze, and when I glance at Anna, her eyes are lit with a devilish gleam.

Shit, I was totally caught staring.

"You're on speaker," Nixon advises.

Even his voice is a huge fucking turn-on. Before Nixon came into my life, voices didn't really do it for me, but I would pay him to read me stories at night. *Hmm... could I add that to the bodyguard package?* I mean, I'm already being forced to have him be a part of my life. I might as well get all the benefits of it. But letting anyone close to me is dangerous. The last thing I need is for the world to find out I've been lying.

"The driveway is clear, but you need to hurry. I'm pretty sure the reporters are tipping off their friends that Dante is coming home today," a male, who must be Denver, reports.

"We're right around the corner. As soon as you see me, open the gate for us and make sure it's closed behind us immediately. After that, do a walk of the perimeter. Make sure no one is trying to climb a wall or anything," Nixon instructs.

"On it," Denver replies, then ends the call.

"Why can't people just leave us alone?" I complain.

Anna squeezes my hand, offering me a warm smile. "Because people are assholes and have nothing better to do."

She isn't wrong. The paparazzi are only doing their job, but I still wish they were more respectful. I try to get them photos when I can. Anna and I even tip people off from time to time when we are making public appearances so they'll leave us alone other times, but it doesn't always work. With a crazy thing like what happened on the red carpet, these people are going to be vultures for at least a couple of weeks before they move on to a new piece of meat.

"Look into my eyes," Anna commands as we pull into the driveway.

I do as I'm told, my lips slowly turning up as she beams at me. "No one out there matters. They are just trying to get a look into your life that they are *not* entitled to. Once we are past the gate, this will be over, and we'll be able to be us again," she assures me, but I'm not sure I believe her.

Nothing is going to be how it used to be.

Someone tried to kill me. The same man who somehow knows I'm gay.

We now have new people in our lives, and I'm not sure if we can truly trust them. So, no, we can't be us again. Not yet, anyway. Because the *us* she is talking about are the people no one gets to see. With Nixon and his crew being around, it's not safe to be us.

"I'm going to work on the security system. After, we can go over your list of people," Nixon tells Anna after we are inside our house.

"Thank you so much."

"Are you sure you want to tell him about Brittany?" I ask quietly as we make our way to the living room, the opposite direction Nixon is heading.

"I'll just say she's a friend," Anna replies, but it's still risky. I'm chewing on my lip when her warm hand lands on my arm, and she stares into my eyes. "Dante, Brittany and I have been together for three years. She already deals with the fact that I'm in the closet and our relationship only exists behind these walls. What do you expect me to do... break up with her because we are now more or less on lockdown?"

I shake my head and plop onto the couch. Anna does the same, landing close to me.

"I'd never ask you to break up with her. You and Brittany are amazing together. But if people find out you're together, they are going to wonder why I'm pretending to date you."

"Just tell them it's to protect me. No one will find out you're gay, I promise," she assures me, her firm eyes on mine, and I want to believe her.

"The guy on the red carpet knew," I remind her.

Her brows pull together, and her lips twist. "But how? We've always been so careful, and you've only ever been with two guys. How could he possibly know?"

"I've been asking myself that same question. I wish I had a better memory. Maybe I could figure out how he possibly came to that conclusion. Was I seeing Jeramiah during the filming of *Music in the Trees*?"

"No, you broke up before then. You wanted to focus on your first big movie," Anna reminds me, triggering a memory.

"But he did come to my trailer one night," I admit.

Anna's eyes shoot open wide, and she gasps. "You didn't tell me that."

"I didn't think it was a big deal. He was begging me to take him back, but I refused. Jeramiah wasn't comfortable being in the closet anymore. Even if I could have balanced a relationship and a big movie, it was unfair to him to be my dirty little secret."

Anna nods with sad eyes. "I understand that a lot," she confesses with a slight tremble in her voice.

"Anna, are you and Britt only staying in the closet for me?" I ask, this sudden realization washing over me.

Why hadn't I come to this conclusion sooner?

Maybe I assumed she wanted to keep it a secret because of her acting career, but by the way she's acting right now, I'm not sure if that's true.

"Maybe," she admits, nibbling on her lower lip. "It wasn't always that way. At first, I didn't want to come out because I was scared it would tank my career, but so many actors and actresses are coming out, and they aren't facing the backlash I was expecting. Don't get me wrong, I've been happy playing the role of your girlfriend, but I kind of want to ask Brittany to marry me."

"Holy shit." I gasp, throwing my head back against the couch. "I'm the worst friend ever."

"No, you're not. I should have spoken up sooner."

I shake my head. "I shouldn't have been a self-centered asshole," I admit. "It's obvious how in love you two are. Just seeing you together almost makes me sick because it's so... nice. If I was a better friend, I would have been pushing you to make it official and end our fake relationship."

"Don't beat yourself up too much. We both could have done better."

"Let's ask Elanor to create a game plan for us to break up."

Anna's face lights up as tear glistens in her eyes. "You'd really do that for me?"

"You're my best friend. I want you to be happy. If that's with Brittany and not me, so be it," I joke.

My best friend launches herself at me and wraps her arms around my shoulders for a tight hug.

"I love you," she whispers.

"I love you too."

"Okay, I'm ready to go over your lists now," Nixon calls out, and I slowly let Anna go before kissing her cheek.

Anna stares into my eyes as if asking permission to tell Nixon the whole story about Brittany. I nod, silently giving my blessing. If she trusts Nixon already, she can obviously tell him anything she wants about herself. I'm not ready to spill my secrets yet. Not sure if I'll ever be.

"We're ready," Anna replies with a giant smile.

I can't believe I was so blinded by what I wanted that I didn't see my best friend was ready for more. But now that we're breaking up, what am I going to do? How am I going to keep prying eyes out of my personal life? Even though Anna is ready to come out of the closet, I am not.

"Do you have a lot of people coming and going from this place?" Nixon asks, sitting across from us in an oversized leather recliner. Most people are swallowed up by it, but it actually looks like it was made for him.

"Not really. We keep a close circle. We only have two people who help with meals and cleaning," Anna supplies. "The main person who is here a lot is my girlfriend, Brittany."

Nixon's expression doesn't change at Anna's admission. I'm impressed by his poker face. *Note to self—don't play card games with that man. He obviously would be able to bluff well.*

"Are you in a poly relationship?" Nixon asks, and Anna and I shake our heads.

"Our relationship is fake," I inform him.

"I wasn't ready to come out of the closet, and Dante wasn't ready to settle down, so creating a fake relationship was something we came up with to keep people away and keep the gossip at a minimum," Anna adds.

I reach between us and squeeze her hand, silently thanking her for not outing me. Not that she would do something like that.

"We are going to be ending our fake relationship soon, though," I explain, filling Nixon in. "Anna and Brittany are ready to make things official soon."

"Congratulations," Nixon tells Anna. "Does anyone know the relationship is fake?"

"Only us and Elanor," Anna answers. "Why?"

"I'm just wondering if that might be the motive behind the drugging."

"What... you think someone tried to kill Dante to be with me?" Anna shrieks, and Nixon shrugs.

"The more I know about your personal lives, the more I can connect the dots," Nixon states.

"You know enough," I bite out.

Nixon narrows his eyes at me at the same time Anna elbows me in the ribs. When I turn, one of her brows is lifted, and her jaw is tight. She's silently warning me to behave, but she knows how I am.

"While we are on this topic, I did want to ask you a few questions about the night of the red carpet." Nixon's expression is more neutral now, but instead of listening to him, I stand, stretching my arms above my head.

"I'm tired. We can do this later," I snap and make my way to my room.

He's going to ask what the nerd said to us, and I'm not sure how I'm going to tell the truth *and* keep my secret at the same time. Would it be the end of the world if one more person knew? Fuck, I don't know. This is all so overwhelming. Too much is happening all at once, and I hate it.

"You forgot your water," Anna calls out, rushing toward me as I reach my door.

"Thanks," I mutter, taking the bottle from her.

"You need to tell him the whole truth," she says.

I sigh. "What if he doesn't keep my secret?"

"Then we sue him for everything he's worth." She gives me a cheeky smirk. "He signed an NDA, and my gut is insisting we can trust him. You know I have amazing intuition."

"I'll consider it," I answer. Once I'm in my room, I collapse onto my bed.

I've known I was gay since I was ten years old, and I have been keeping it a secret ever since. I've only ever told a handful of people, so adding another to the mix is a big step for me. If Nixon doesn't keep his mouth shut, everything will change in my life. I'm not sure I'm ready for that to happen.

Chapter 4

Nixon

AFTER A SHORT KNOCK on Sophy's door, I enter our computer wizard's office without waiting for a response. We're kind of past the need for that. Knocking is more a heads-up that someone is entering around here and less a way to ask permission to enter. "Have you been able to dig up anything on the guy from the red carpet?" I ask without a greeting, antsy and eager for new information.

She looks up from her computer, pushes her purple heart-shaped glasses up her nose, and shakes her head, her red hair falling around her face. "It's not like we have much to go on," she replies. "We've got a name that's fake. A company that is real but never had a Barney Anderson working for them. And somehow, not a single picture of him. How the hell is that possible?" She sighs, clearly as frustrated as I am.

I've been wondering the exact same thing. We've been working on this case for four solid days but are only hitting dead ends. With such a high-profile client, this shouldn't be possible.

"There are details Dante is holding from us, but I can't force him to open up."

"Would either Anna or Dante be willing to meet with Slate to get a drawing of the guy?" Sophy inquires, mentioning her boyfriend, an amazing forensic sketch artist. "I could upload the image and run it through my software. Maybe this guy will pop up somewhere."

When Sophy first started dating Slate, I was happy she found someone she clicked with so quickly. The fact that he's able to assist the company from time to time is an added bonus.

"Great idea, Soph. I'll contact Anna right away. Dante is a no-go, but Anna would gladly help wherever possible. Call Slate and send me the dates he's free."

She nods, and after I exit her office, I make my way to my own, pulling out my cell and firing off a text.

Me: *Would you be able to give a good description of the guy from the red carpet? We have a forensic sketch artist we use from time to time, and if we can get an image, we should be able to run it through our database to try and find this guy.*

Anna: *I'm in. Name the time and place. I'm not back at work for another two weeks.*

Me: *Perfect. Once I get his schedule, I'll let you know.*

Anna: *Thanks!*

Me: *No problem. I'll be in touch soon.*

Anna: *Oh... Also, I'll be out for the evening. Not sure if I need to tell you that or not, but I'm heading over to Brittany's house. I'll be back tomorrow afternoon. I already let Knox know, and he'll be escorting me over there.*

I'm happy to hear she's following the rules and keeping in contact with the bodyguard we assigned her.

Me: *Thanks for the heads up.*

I hit send, place my phone on my desk, open a few emails, and relay information to different team members.

Business is booming, and it's almost time for me to stop taking on clients myself, but the idea of being behind a desk *every day* makes my skin itch. At least right now I have a full-time client with a pretty easy schedule, even if he is a brat who seems to love to get on my nerves.

The day is busy, and I feel dead on my feet by the time I get home. Nothing a hot shower can't fix, though.

I make my way to my bedroom, strip, and head directly into the shower, turning it to a scalding temperature in an attempt to wash away the stress of the day.

Once I'm clean, I step out, ready to climb into bed and pass out. But unfortunately, that won't be possible because my phone vibrates and rings on the counter.

Buzz, buzz. Ding, dong, ding.

It's an alert I set specifically for Dante's alarm system.

I rush to pick it up, glare at the notification, and charge into my room to get dressed.

"Alexa, call Dante Michaelson," I shout as I open a drawer to grab a pair of pants.

The speaker rings and rings *and rings* before going to voicemail.

"For fuck's sake," I mutter. "Alexa, call Denver."

"What's up?" Denver answers straight away.

"I'm on my way to Dante Michaelson's house. There was an alert that someone has entered the property. I checked the cameras, but I don't recognize the vehicle. It's not on the list, and Dante isn't answering his phone."

"Do you need backup?" Denver asks.

"I don't think so, but I wanted you on alert nonetheless."

"Sounds good. Keep me updated."

We end the call, and as fast as humanly possible, I get ready and rush over to Dante's house, calling him three more times along the way. The only reason I'm not bringing in a full team and the police is the fact that the unknown driver didn't force entry. He was let in by Dante. Considering he loves to fight me on everything, I can see this as him breaking the rules to spite me.

As I'm pulling into the driveway, the vehicle is exiting, and I stop in front, blocking their only way out.

"Who are you?" I shout as I get out of my car, making my way to the other driver's door.

"I'm just a delivery guy," he yells. "If you're some jealous boyfriend, I don't have time for this shit. Can you get out of my way?"

It's then my eyes zero in on the sign in his window, stating clearly that he is a delivery driver, and I *almost* feel like an ass.

"Sorry," I say and move my car out of the way. The second the driver is gone, I head up the driveway.

My jaw aches from how hard I'm clenching it as I climb the steps to the house. I'm fucking pissed. Not that Dante ordered takeout but that he didn't answer any of my calls or give me a heads-up first. He *knows* the rules and is deliberately being an ass.

After slamming my fist against the door three times, I wait for Dante to answer. I could let myself in, but I have respect for people, unlike some douchey celebrity clients.

"Did I forget something?" he asks before sucking in a breath when he realizes it's me. "What the hell are you doing here?" His eyes hold so much fire behind them, and if I didn't know he was straight, I would think a hint of lust as well.

"If you'd answer your phone, you'd know." I sneer, trying not to dwell on what lies behind those eyes.

"I ordered takeout, for fuck's sake. I didn't think I needed to make my babysitter aware of that." He scoffs and stalks away from me.

Everything in me is screaming to grab him and demand some respect, but that would be crossing a line, and I don't want to lose Dante as a client, even though he frustrates me beyond belief.

"All I ask is that you keep me informed. I'm trying to keep you alive here. Or do you want to die?"

"Of course, I don't want to fucking die," he yells, turning on his heels and glaring at me. This time, the look is pure rage, the hint of anything else gone. "But I also don't want people all up in my business. Why the hell is it such a big deal for a person to want to keep to themselves?"

"Keep to yourself all you want, but it's my job to make sure someone doesn't try to kill you again. You make that really fucking hard when you refuse to follow basic instructions."

"I'm your boss, not the other way around. Get that through your fucking head or take a hike," he screams.

"Fire me, then," I challenge, knowing he won't. He's simply being a stubborn ass. I take a step forward, going toe to toe with him, needing to show him I won't be pushed around.

"You have no idea how badly I want to." He snarls, staring directly into my eyes.

His breathing is a little labored, and his eyes are dilating a bit. There is a hint of lust again, but that doesn't make sense. It's probably from how angry he is.

"I'm not trying to control your life here, but I need you to stop acting like a fucking brat for just a moment and listen to me."

"Maybe I like being a brat," he counters, his eyes sparkling with mischievous energy I love in a partner. But he isn't mine, so I take a step away before I do something stupid.

"I see that," I mutter, trying to get myself under control. "Clearly, you don't care about your own safety, but you do care about your friends. So if you aren't going to do it for yourself, do it for them. Stop challenging me every step of the way and meet me halfway here."

Dante glares at me for a second before sighing. "Fine. I'll text you next time I order takeout," he concedes.

"All I'm asking is for you to keep me in the loop. I'm not the bad guy here," I remind him, but he rolls his eyes. My fingers twitch at my side, but I somehow keep my feet frozen where they are.

"Everyone is a bad guy. Some are just better at hiding it than others," he states, grabs his pizza off the counter, and walks away.

THE DRIVE TO THE lot where Dante is filming his newest movie isn't too long from his house, but the energy in the vehicle is tense. Probably because Dante doesn't want me with him today. He made it clear last night that he doesn't trust me and would gladly fire me if everyone in his life wasn't insisting he have protection.

"Are you excited for your first day back on set?" Elanor asks Dante in the back seat of my SUV.

"I'd be happier if I didn't have a babysitter trailing behind me," he grumbles.

I clench my jaw. I hate when he calls me his babysitter. My job is so much more important than that. But the fact that he constantly acts like a toddler around me makes the title suit the situation.

Today has just started, and I already know it's going to be long as fuck.

"I'm sorry that you're so famous now and need personal security when you aren't at home. Maybe I should get you blacklisted instead, and you can return to a normal life," Elanor teases.

"Stop being a smartass," Dante scolds her.

Even though my eyes are on the road, the smile in his voice is evident.

"Do you need a reminder of your schedule this week?" Elanor asks, changing the subject.

"Five long-ass days, one off, three even *longer* days, two off, rinse and repeat for the next three months," Dante replies, coaxing a giggle out of Elanor.

"More or less. Stop acting so put off by it. This is the part you actually love."

"You're not wrong there," he murmurs.

It doesn't take us too long to get to the studio, where I show my credentials and gain access to the parking lot.

"Find a bench to sit on and stay out of my way," Dante spits out at me when we arrive at our location, but I shake my head, refusing to let him get under my skin.

"No can do, buttercup," I tease. I absolutely enjoy the way his jaw tightens and his lips purse at the nickname. *Maybe I should use that one often.* "My eyes are on you all day long," I state firmly after I'm able to stop staring at his mouth. "Where you go, I go. Get used to having a shadow."

He glares at me briefly before spinning on his heels and heading to his trailer. Thankfully not arguing any further.

"Sorry about him," Elanor says as we follow him.

"Got any tips on how I can get him to soften up to me? It would be a lot easier on everyone if he stopped fighting me so much."

She presses her lips together and stares at her shoe. "I wish I had an answer, but unfortunately, he's going to be like this until you earn his trust."

"How do I do that?"

She shakes her head with her lips pressed together. "I don't actually know. Time, I guess."

"Great," I mutter, leaning against the trailer to wait for Dante to finish changing.

I'm not sure how much time passes when the trailer door flies open, and Dante stomps toward the set. I follow him as he bitches about how much he doesn't need me.

As promised, much to his disappointment, I stay close to where he is acting. I make sure to stay out of the way, and I'll admit it's a lot more entertaining than I thought it would be. I figured I'd be bored out of my mind sitting on the sidelines, but I'm intrigued by everything going on.

"And... cut!" the director yells after a few scenes. "Take five, everyone."

Dante stands from his crouched position, smiles at another actor, and heads toward me.

He's dripping in sweat from running around nonstop. My eyes are drawn to his ripped chest as it rises and falls with his labored breaths.

"Would you like a glass of water?" a young woman with a giant smile and hearts in her eyes asks Dante, but I step in before he can accept it.

"I've got his water here," I tell her as nicely as possible and place a sealed bottle in Dante's hand.

"Oh... uh... sorry..." she stammers before rushing away.

"Way to ruin her day," Dante goads me.

"Just trying to keep you alive. You know... *my job*," I respond with a tight-lipped smile.

"It's a glass of water," he complains, then opens his bottle and guzzles the drink.

My eyes act like they have a mind of their own and track his Adam's apple as it rises and falls while he downs the cold beverage. I bite the inside of my cheek to stop myself from getting aroused at such a simple image.

"Yeah, it's just a glass of water, but it was also a simple shot that almost killed you a week ago," I remind him after I stop staring.

"Whatever," he mumbles before finishing the bottle.

"Do you need anything else?" I ask.

This time, his eyes meet mine, and he stares at me so intently that it makes my heart race. Neither of us glances away.

"Another bottle of water," he replies, pulling us from whatever the fuck was happening.

I grab another bottle from the cooler I had brought over a little while ago and hand it to him. He nods in thanks, which is apparently all I'll be getting. But at least it's better than biting my head off.

The rest of the day flies by, and after filming has ended, Dante and I make our way to his trailer.

"People want to go out for drinks," he tells me, and while I appreciate him volunteering his plans, something is off.

"I thought you kept a close circle," I point out, and he rolls his eyes.

Does he have any idea how often he does that? Or the fact that it makes my hand twitch every time?

"I do. But it's also not a bad idea to build good relations with people I work with often."

I guess he has a point, but the idea doesn't sit well with me. "Where are they planning on hanging out?" I question, trying to weigh the pros and cons here.

"Some bar called Magic." He spreads his fingers out and moves his hands along with the word, almost making me laugh, but the unease settling in my gut takes over, and I don't even break a smile.

"I don't think it's the best plan," I state. "It's only been a week since someone tried to *kill* you, Dante. It's best to keep a low profile for the time being. Everyone knows you are working on this film. If word gets out that you are out for drinks, it won't be hard for anyone to find where you are. It's too risky."

Dante stops, closes his eyes, and takes a deep inhale before slowly letting it out. When his eyes open again, landing on mine, there is tenacious energy behind them.

"I was *telling* you I'm going for drinks with my colleagues because you asked me to keep you in the loop," he states firmly, never breaking eye contact. "I wasn't asking for permission. So you can either tag along like a good little puppy or fuck off. I don't care either way." With those words, he turns and climbs into his trailer, slamming the door in my face.

So much for making progress.

While Dante changes, I make a call to Knox. Anna isn't going out tonight, so he's free. I tell him to meet us at Magic and inform the establishment about who is on their way. I'm sure the other actors' assistants have already done that, but Dante doesn't have an assistant, so I'm doubling as that tonight.

Part of me wonders if he's going out tonight to build connections or if he's doing it to prove some sort of a point. So after I've lined Knox up, I call Elanor.

"What's up?" she says by way of greeting.

"Dante has decided he wants to hang out with his coworkers tonight," I inform her. "What's his alcohol tolerance like?"

"None. He barely drinks. This doesn't sound like Dante at all. Did something happen?"

I take a moment to recall the entire day. "Shit," I mutter as something stands out from right before filming ended.

"What?" Elanor demands.

"Dante and Anna's breakup went live today. An actor was making fun of Dante for it. I didn't hear the entire conversation, but it pissed Dante off. Maybe he's trying to make some sort of point." My earlier thoughts start to ring truer as I connect the dots. "Can you talk to him? Try and get him to reconsider? I'm a bodyguard. I'll keep him safe, but I saw how freaked out he was at the hospital when he thought word was going to get out about the drugs. His image is important to him. If he gets drunk tonight, that could affect more than he's maybe thinking about right now."

"Give him the phone," Elanor states in a no-bullshit tone, so I knock on the trailer.

"What?" Dante growls out, flinging the door open with a pissed-off expression.

"Phone's for you." I hold out my cell.

"Hello?" he answers, narrowing his eyes at me.

I'm not sure what Elanor says, but it makes him sigh, and he shuts the trailer door again. It's a bit of a wait for Dante to finish his conversation, but once he has, he opens the door, shoving my phone at me.

"Thanks for tattling on me," he grumbles as he stalks past me.

"What's the plan?" I ask, following him to my SUV.

"Take me home," he says dryly, the irritation evident.

I nod and text Knox, alerting him to the change in plans.

"Would you like to stop anywhere first?" I inquire when we're in the car.

"Actually, I'd like a pizza if that won't get me murdered," he bites out.

Back to this again, great. I don't argue, not wanting to fight.

"What kind? Do you have a preference for locations?"

He rattles off his order, and after I call it in, I head toward the address.

The drive is quiet. I almost feel bad for Dante. Part of me wants to know where his head is at. The other part of me is aware it's none of my business, so I don't pry. However, it also serves as a great reminder that I can't let myself get close to Dante. If I do, it will lead us down a far too dangerous path for my liking.

Chapter 5

Dante

Nixon places my pizza on the counter. "Do you need anything else?" he asks with a kind, formal voice that actually irritates me further.

"Yeah," I reply, crossing my arms over my chest, realizing a little too late that it makes me look like a petulant child. "I need you to stop fucking with my life. If I want to mess everything up, that's my prerogative."

Leaning against the island counter, he raises a brow at me. It pisses me off even more *and* turns me on at the same time. *Fuck, this man is aggravating.*

"If you actually wanted to fuck everything up, you'd be out right now. You don't care what I say."

I drop my arms, balling my hands into fists at my sides, almost ready to release all my pent-up frustration.

"Are you always such a know-it-all?" I bite out, not letting go quite yet.

The moment I take the lid off this bottled-up anger, shit will hit the fan, and I'm not sure I'm ready for that yet.

"I'm just pointing out the obvious." He sighs and runs his hand over his face like he's had enough of my shit or something.

"Oh, I'm obvious, am I? Well, if I'm so see-through, tell me more about me, then."

"You're a spoiled rotten brat who has had everything handed to you on a silver platter since making a name for yourself," Nixon starts, leaning toward me with fire in his eyes. "You had every little detail of your life planned out to a T, but getting drugged has tipped your world on its side, and you don't know how to handle it anymore. To you, everything feels like it's up in the air right now, and all of the little things are setting you off. You're letting people push your buttons when you would normally let it roll off your back. And even though you're pissed at me for calling Elanor, you're also grateful. You're just too proud to admit it. You act like you hate me, but the truth of the matter is, I'm just an easy target to take your rattled emotions out on."

Well, shit, he actually hit most of it on the head. How does he do that? Clearly, Elanor did find the best when she hired Nixon, but I won't be letting that secret out of the bag. I'm good at keeping my mouth shut when I want to.

"You don't fucking know anything." I scoff and make my way to the other side of the island to grab a plate.

"Really? What part did I get wrong?"

"All of it," I lie, and Nixon laughs. He actually fucking laughs, which makes the anger in my veins that's been simmering under the surface boil.

"I thought you were an amazing actor. How are you such a shit liar?" he goads.

"Well, you're an asshole."

"You're not wrong. But I own my shit, unlike brats like you."

"Well, we've already discussed how I like being a brat, so what are you going to do about it?" I challenge, but the undertone to my question is different. There isn't a bite like I normally have when I'm talking to Nixon.

"If you were mine, you'd be over my knee already with a bright red ass, making it hard for you to sit for a week," he states before pushing off the counter and stalking toward the door. "I'll be back in the morning. Don't do anything stupid in the meantime."

My cock is hard, and I'm glad I'm standing behind the island where he can't see how turned on I am by the idea of being spanked.

"I've never been very kinky, but I kind of want Brittany to spank me now," Anna says, coming down the hall from where she was obviously spying.

"Is my life entertainment for you?" I question, grabbing the plate I meant to get a while ago.

"Obviously," she teases with a giant grin. "I kind of want to call off my flight to Paris next week so I can stay around and witness everything unfurl here."

"Well, I'm glad I make your life less boring." I scoff as I plate up two pieces of pizza.

"Why are you so hard on him?" Anna asks, pulling out a slice of pizza without worrying about a plate.

"He just gets under my skin," I lie.

Anna giggles and takes a bite of her pizza. "And it has nothing to do with the fact that he's super hot?"

I glare at her. "Obviously, he's attractive, but he's not my type."

Anna laughs harder. "Babe, he's *exactly* what you need in a man. He puts you in your place, and while you love pushing back, you also enjoy how controlling he is."

"Stop living in my head," I whine before heading toward the living room.

"You should open up that you're gay. Maybe you can have an employee-with-benefits relationship on the side." Anna waggles her brows at me as she plops down next to me on the couch.

"What if he isn't gay?"

Anna shoots me an are-you-being-serious look.

"I don't think straight men threaten to spank other men," she mocks, and she isn't wrong there.

I chew on my pizza, pondering her words, when she asks the question I figured was coming. "What happened today? Elanor texted me about you wanting to go out for drinks. That isn't like you. You're a homebody through and through."

"Jason Millsworth made a comment about our breakup," I whisper, avoiding eye contact with my best friend.

"What did that twatwaffle say?" Anna almost growls.

"That you were too good for me. Said he wasn't sure how I kept you for as long as I did. Went on and on about how I probably wouldn't be able to pick up a girl if I tried. I'm not sure why it got to me. Everyone knows he's a womanizer, and there are even rumors he's abusive. His opinion shouldn't mean anything to me, but it got under my skin today. I guess it's just a mixture of everything."

"I'm sorry, babe." She leans over to kiss my cheek. "Maybe we could have picked a better time to do this breakup."

I shake my head. "When would be a better time? It's probably for the best that everything is happening all at once. I just wasn't planning on trying to figure out what I want in life right now. I knew it would be something I had to come to terms with eventually but wasn't expecting it to be now. Which is pathetic, isn't it? I'm twenty-four. I should know what I want in life, but I don't." I let out a dry laugh, accompanied by a few tears. "I wish I was strong like you."

Anna takes my plate, puts it on the coffee table, and wraps her arms around me. "We all take our journey at different paces. What's right for one isn't always right for the next person. I know why you've stayed in the closet for as long as you have, and if that's where you want to stay for now, that's okay."

My phone buzzes in my pocket, pulling my attention from Anna. The moment I see the caller ID, I sigh.

"It's like we thought of them and made them call," I whisper, showing Anna the screen. She grimaces when she sees who it is.

I take a deep breath before answering the phone on speaker. Anna needs to be privy to this conversation, I'm sure.

"Hi, Mom."

"I just heard about the red carpet." She snivels on the other end of the line. "Are you okay?"

"Um... yeah, I'm fine. It was a week ago now. I've almost forgotten about it," I lie.

"Well, I'm glad, baby. I would have flown out there, but life gets busy," she states.

Everything has always been more important than me in my parents' life. I'm used to it by now, but it doesn't make it suck any less.

I'm pretty sure the only reason they had me was because it was what everyone else wanted for them, to build that perfect fairy-tale life. I'm sure they would have had more kids they didn't care about if it wasn't for the complications Mom had when she gave birth to me, leading to her having a hysterectomy afterward.

"Is there anything else you need, Mom? I've got to be up early in the morning for work."

"Oh, right. Your father still wishes you would quit that sinful job."

I shoot Anna a look and stick my finger toward my mouth, pretending to gag.

"Well, that isn't happening. So was there something else you needed?"

"We also heard about your breakup." I'm sure *that's* the real reason she called. "Are you sure you are done-done? Anna is such a sweet young lady. We were hoping you'd get married soon."

"Sorry, Mom. It's over. Anna and I are still friends, but we don't love each other that way anymore," I say, giving her my rehearsed line.

"What if you fly home for a few days? I could introduce you to a few new members of the church."

I clench my jaw. "You know I'm not religious. That probably wouldn't be the best idea." Anna squeezes my hand.

"Honey, don't you think you should reconsider that? Jesus loves you," she tells me like she has a hundred times.

"That's how you feel, Mom, but I'm not changing my stance on this."

"I'll pray for you," she states and ends the call.

No 'I love you.' No checking to see how I'm actually doing. Only filling an agenda, like always.

My father doesn't talk to me because I turned away from the church. He told me it wasn't becoming of a pastor's son to turn his back on God. I would love to see what he'd have to say if I ever told him I'm gay. I'm sure I would be completely cut off at that point. Even though I don't have the best relationship with my mom, it still terrifies me to think she would outcast me for something I can't control.

"Your parents suck." Anna lays her head on my shoulder.

I rest my chin on her head and sigh. "At least yours are amazing."

She smiles. "They really are. They're nervous about me coming out publicly but will stand behind me if I'm ready."

"When are you doing that?" I ask, my stomach turning a little.

"Not for a while. I don't want the world to think I moved on too quickly," Anna replies with a wink, easing my anxiety a bit. "My parents were asking if you wanted to find a boyfriend now."

I shake my head. "It wouldn't be fair to anyone as long as I'm still in the closet."

We stay silent for a while, curled up on the couch together before my eyelids get heavy.

"It's time for bed," I say, then stretch and let out a giant yawn.

"I think I was half asleep on your shoulder," Anna mumbles.

I chuckle. "I've got comfortable shoulders."

"Before you go to bed, I want to ask you something." I nod for her to continue. "If things were different, would you *want* a boyfriend?"

A yearning stirs inside me, and I nod. "Yeah, I think I would... but it's not possible." Sighing, I run a hand over my face.

"I'm going to say something I've wanted to say for a long time. Just don't hate me, okay?"

"I promise I won't hate you."

"Would it really be the end of the world if your parents shut you out? They already treat you like shit. Why do you even want them in your life? I mean, I get that they are your family, which makes this really hard, but I'm also your family. Maybe sometimes a family you *choose* is better than the one you are born with. If they push you away, I'll always be here."

I wrap my arms around her and bury my face in her hair as I cry.

"I'm just scared," I confess.

She nods, rubbing my back. "I get it, babe, but I'm here. I promise. You won't be alone, no matter what you choose. I'm always here for you."

We hold each other for a few minutes before deciding that it really is time to go to bed. But sleep isn't easy to come by tonight. A million thoughts flitter around my brain like butterflies swarming a field of flowers.

Am I really happy with the life I'm living right now? Or am I ready to say fuck the consequences and live my life for me?

Chapter 6

Nixon

THE WEEK HAS FLOWN by. Thankfully, for the most part, Dante and I have fallen into a routine. He's still a brat with a sharp tongue, but he doesn't push me as hard as he used to, and he isn't making reckless decisions that put his safety at risk.

"Could I ask you a few more questions about the red-carpet night?" I ask Dante when I pull into his driveway.

"Haven't I told you everything already?" He groans with the same attitude he always has when he talks to me. At least he's consistent. I'll give him that.

"That's the thing. I don't think you have. My team is busting their asses trying to figure out who the hell this guy is and why he wanted to kill you, but if you aren't a hundred percent honest with me, then we can't help you." I turn around to look at him in the back seat after I put the car in park.

"Fine, come in and ask your questions," he grumbles, then gets out of the car and rushes to his front door.

Well, shit. I kind of expected him to put up more of a fight.

"What do you want to know?" he asks, pouring himself a glass of wine when I join him in the kitchen.

"You drink wine?"

He scoffs. "I might not be a *big* drinker, but I do have the occasional drink here and there."

I nod. "Makes sense. If you didn't drink at all, you wouldn't have taken that shot," I supply. "Okay, there are a few things that aren't making sense to me," I start while Dante sips his drink. As he lowers the glass, my focus is drawn to his lips and the way he licks them clean.

Fuck, Dante is too distracting. He's making this job so damn hard—among other things.

"What's not making sense? It's all pretty black and white to me. He asked us some questions, we took a shot, he drugged me, end of story," Dante rattles off, snippy and put off.

"Yeah, I've got that, but *what* questions did he ask? Did he make any weird comments? Did he say something that was way out of the ordinary? I need more, Dante."

Dante stares at me for a moment before taking a deep inhale and slowly blowing it out.

"What I'm about to tell you doesn't leave these walls. I don't care if it will benefit your team," he states, staring intently into my eyes. The usual fire that lurks there is missing, replaced with insecurity.

"I promise. If it's information they need, I'll figure out a way to notify them without spilling your secrets. Whatever you say right now won't ever leave my lips."

"When we made our way to him, he said it was nice to meet me *again.* I don't recall meeting him, but he told me we met on the *Music in the Trees* set four years ago. You've seen what a set can be like. It's filled with hundreds of people that I'll never remember. When I apologized for not recognizing him, he looked upset."

"Upset or angry?"

"Upset. Like he really thought I would remember him, but I have no idea why."

"Okay, what else?"

"He had a stack of index cards to ask us questions for the game. He used them for Anna's question, but he went off script for mine."

I'm thankful he's finally opening up. This is all helpful information and would have been nice to have weeks ago. It's beyond frustrating that he wouldn't just tell me all this from the beginning, but I guess I should be grateful I have it now.

We tried to run the sketch Slate did through all our databases but kept coming up short. Whoever this guy is doesn't have a prior history with the police. Without knowing where to look next, we didn't have anything else to compare his picture against. But knowing he worked on the *Music in the Trees* set, we might be able to find something now.

"What did he ask you?" I push, hoping Dante isn't about to close off.

"What does it matter?" He scoffs, picks up his wine glass, and walks past me toward the living room.

"It could give us a motive," I tell him, trailing behind him.

Dante sets the glass on the coffee table and sits on the large couch. I take a seat in the oversized recliner and wait for him to talk. If I keep pushing, he'll shut down completely, and we won't be much better off than we were before this conversation started.

"He asked when did I know I was gay," he whispers.

My brows shoot up before I have a chance to cool my expression. I'm not normally caught off guard, but that isn't what I was expecting him to say. But now it makes total sense as to why he wasn't being forthright with the information.

"Anna was a pro and played it off, but the way he was staring at me told me it wasn't a hunch. He knew the truth, but I don't know *how* he knew. I've been extremely careful to never let that secret out."

"Were you seeing anyone at the time of the filming?" I ask, trying to help Dante come up with the answers he doesn't have.

"I broke up with my boyfriend just before. He wanted me to come out of the closet. I wasn't ready. Hell, it's been four years, and I'm still not sure I'm ready," he admits, throwing his head back against the couch. "So many things are confusing me about that night, though. Like if he knew I was gay, why try to kill me? Wouldn't it be smarter to blackmail me?"

I nod. That exact thought had crossed my mind.

"Did you ever hook up with anyone while filming *Music in the Trees*? Maybe even hug a man too long or kiss someone?"

Dante ponders the question before sitting up again.

"My ex visited me on set one night. We were in my trailer, and he begged me to take him back. He kissed me before he left. But no one else was in there with us. I'm not stupid."

"Were your blinds completely closed? Could someone possibly peek inside?"

Dante nibbles on his lower lip and shrugs. "I guess it's a possibility. Do you think the dork from the red carpet saw us kiss?"

"I'm not entirely sure, but it could be something. Was there anyone on the set who was overly attentive to you? Maybe someone who constantly brought you water or snacks or wanted to get on your good side?"

"I should tell you now, I have the world's worst memory when it comes to that shit," he admits. "Nothing sticks out off the top of my head."

I nod, wishing we had something else. It still feels like there is a puzzle piece missing here.

"So, did me spilling my darkest secret help you at all?"

I shrug. "It gives us more places to look and more things to think about. Thanks for opening up to me."

"Not like I had much choice," he mutters.

"You always have a choice, Dante."

He scoffs. "Really? Because I *wish* I had a choice in my life right now. I don't tell people about my sexuality *ever*. Someone found out even with how careful I am, and they want me dead over it. Now I'm forced to have more people in my life who could possibly find out about who I am, then what? Will they want me dead too? Is being gay that fucking bad?" His voice breaks before his anger returns. "So if any of that seems like I have a choice, you're clearly missing something."

"I wasn't trying to push you to come out," I reassure him. "I had no fucking idea. I thought maybe he had caught you sleeping with another woman. I mean, it would make sense that you wanted to scratch an itch seeing as you and Anna weren't really together. I thought maybe the guy was a jealous ex or something. I'm sorry I pressured you into telling me." I grab the back of my neck and stand. "Do you need to go anywhere tomorrow?"

He shakes his head, not looking at me.

"Then I'll see you the day after," I say and leave.

Fuck. I feel like a class-A douche for forcing him out of the closet like that. But I wasn't lying about not having a clue.

Clearly, Dante Michaelson truly is a good actor.

ONCE I GET TO work, I head directly to Sophy's office and knock on her door. "Got anything?" I ask.

She shakes her head. "Not yet. I've been sending the sketch to all the people who were in charge of *Music in the Trees,* but it was four years ago. If he was just a small temp worker, it could be that no one remembers him," she supplies.

"Yeah, that's what I was afraid of. This guy is good at laying low, being a person that people don't see, which makes him extra dangerous."

"Why do you think he wants Dante dead?"

"There are a million reasons. Maybe he was pissed that he didn't make an impression on him. Maybe he's delusional. I won't be able to answer that question until we find him."

The response satisfies Sophy, who nods her head.

"If I find anything, I'll let you know," she tells me, and I make my way to my office.

I'm three emails away from clearing my inbox when my phone vibrates across my desk.

Dante: *Hey, babysitter... I need to run to the store. With all of the crazy shit going on, I forgot that Anna's birthday is in two days. I don't have a present for her.*

Me: *When do you want to go?*

Dante: *Now.*

Me: *Great manners that you got there. I'll be at your place in thirty minutes.*

Dante: *Make it twenty. I've got things I need to do.*

I don't bother responding. Instead, I exit out of my computer and let everyone know I'll be busy for the rest of the afternoon. Knowing Dante, this won't be a quick trip. Honestly, I wouldn't put it past him to make me take him to extra stores simply to annoy the shit out of me.

On my way to my car, I take a deep, settling breath, preparing myself for what could be a long day. Thankfully, it doesn't take me long to get to Dante's house, and I don't have time to let my thoughts go off track. Being Dante's bodyguard and having to be in close proximity to him after finding out he's gay is a temptation I can't afford. He's a client.

At least, that's my new mantra.

After picking him up, he doesn't let on as to what the plan is. It turns out that it's exactly as I expected when we get to the mall. He totes me from store to store, and it's testing my patience.

"Anna doesn't really strike me as someone who wants lingerie from her best friend for her birthday," I mutter.

"Then you don't know Anna," Dante responds, then makes me follow him to not one, not two, but three lingerie stores before deciding nothing was good enough for her.

"Do *you* even know Anna at all?" I ask after leaving three more stores.

Dante smirks at me. That mischievous glint behind his eye tells me he has been fucking with me this entire time.

"I bet the next store will have the perfect thing," he declares, but at this point, I'm almost convinced he already has the gift bought, and he is trying to get me to quit.

Thankfully, the next stop is the Apple Store.

"Can I help you?" an associate asks, and Dante nods.

"I have an Apple Watch set aside for Michael Storm," he tells the guy, who nods and rushes to get the item.

My jaw ticks as I fight the urge to strangle Dante. *What a little shit.* We literally spent *hours* looking for a gift that was waiting here for us all along.

"Why do you enjoy fucking with me so much?" I growl into his ear, noticing the way his body responds.

He moves slightly as a shiver runs down his spine, and his lips part as a slight woosh of air escapes.

He's your client, I remind myself, biting the inside of my cheek *hard* to force myself to stay on track.

"It's just so much fun watching that vein throb between your eyebrows," Dante responds with a megawatt grin.

"Here you go, Mr. Storm," the associate says with a smile, handing Dante the Apple Watch, which must already have been paid for.

"Thank you." He accepts the small bag, then turns and walks out.

"Why didn't you get it shipped to your house?" I ask as we make our way out of the mall.

"It would have taken too long, and I wouldn't have been able to mess with you all afternoon."

I take a deep breath, trying to calm myself while *dying* to discipline him. This brat needs a tamer, but there are a million reasons why I can't be it.

Chapter 7

ANNA OPENS HER PRESENT while listening to my story about how I got it and shrieks. "You did what?"

"I was bored. I figured, why not fuck with my bodyguard for the day? Ten out of ten would recommend," I joke with a smirk.

"You are such a little shit." She gives my shoulder a shove. "I'm going to miss you like crazy." The pout on her pink lips is adorable, but I feel the same way.

"Stop picking up contracts for movies so far away from me," I whine and pull her in for a hug.

"I hate being away from everyone I love. At least Brittany gets to come along as my assistant."

"Lucky bitch," I murmur, but there is no bite in my words.

She truly is lucky, and I'm jealous. Anna's life is falling into place perfectly. I wish I could gain the courage to do the same.

What would it be like to have someone to come home to after a long day?

To travel with when I have to film at different locations or do press junkets.

To have someone to share all the highs and lows with.

And, of course, someone to fuck my brains out. It's been so goddamn long since I've had sex with another person. I'm honestly not even sure if I'd be good at it anymore.

"Promise me you won't push Nixon too hard while I'm gone," Anna pleads.

"I make no such promise," I joke.

She groans. "You're the worst. He's going to quit if you don't stop all your antics."

"I highly doubt that. If he were going to quit, he'd have done it by now. Besides, my self-defense mechanism is a smart mouth. I can't even help it."

The look Anna shoots me tells me she sees through my bullshit.

"What am I going to do when you're gone?" I complain. "Elanor isn't the same to talk to."

"I'll only be a phone call away," she reminds me.

I pout. "Yes, but the time difference will be crazy."

"We'll get through it. We always do."

I nod and pull her in for another hug, not wanting her to leave.

I hate when we are apart for work, but the even scarier thought is, eventually, she's going to move out, and I won't have her here all the time.

What am I going to do then?

"CAN I ASK YOU some more questions?" Nixon asks, pulling into my driveway.

I'm supposed to be at some event tonight, but I decided to bail at the last minute. I know I'll face the wrath of Elanor tomorrow when she finds out I didn't show, but that's a tomorrow Dante problem.

It's been three days since Anna left for Paris, and I already miss her like crazy. I'm ridiculously lonely in this big house all by myself, so the idea of hanging out with Nixon, even to answer questions, is inviting. But I can't let Nixon know how eager I am.

"What more do you need from me?" I groan as I unbuckle my seat belt.

"I'm trying to connect the dots. Anything and everything you're willing to tell me would be appreciated."

"What is this, therapy?" I ask as we get out of the car and head to the front door.

As usual, Nixon is right on my tail. "No offense, but you would make a shitty shrink." I can't resist poking the bear.

Nixon blows out a big breath, and I have to bite my tongue to stop the smile that wants to spread across my face. *Fuck, I love getting him going.*

"Want anything to drink?" I ask, making my way to the refrigerator.

"Water's fine," he responds, and I grab two bottles of sparkling water.

"You seriously drink this shit?" he grumbles.

I gasp, placing my hand on my chest in mock surprise. "You don't?"

I already know from studying him that he only drinks plain water, but I won't tell him that.

"Just give me a glass. I'll drink tap water like a normal person." He groans.

"Like a caveman," I quip, then reach for a cup and fill it with the chilled, filtered water from the refrigerator.

"So, what else do you want to know?" I question as I head to the living room and plop onto my favorite couch. "I'm pretty sure I already told you everything that's of any importance."

"How many boyfriends have you had over the years?" he asks.

"Two. I haven't dated anyone since Jeramiah, the guy I broke up with just before *Music in the Trees*."

"Any casual hookups?" he pries, frustrating me.

Deciding to fuck with him, I lean forward. "Do you also want to know what turns me on?" I counter with a smirk.

"Fuck, can't you make anything easy?" he grumbles.

"No casual hookups. I haven't had sex in over four years. Anything else?" I bite out.

"Who all knows about your secret?"

At least that is an easy answer. "Jeramiah and Montgomery, my two exes, Elanor, Brittany, Anna, and her parents. That's it."

"What about your family?"

I laugh so hard my ribs hurt. "Didn't you do a background search before you took me on as a client?" He shrugs. "Do you really think the pastor of a mega-church would have any relationship with their child if he knew he was gay? Not that Daddy dearest has much of a relationship with me these days since I turned my back on God."

"Is that why you stay in the closet?" he asks with a sympathetic look that pisses me off.

"Storytime is over. I'm going to bed," I state right before the power goes out.

Nixon curses. "Stay close," he commands, and for once in my life, I do as I'm told.

"Why the hell did the power go out? It's not like there is a storm or anything."

"Exactly why you need to stay close," he repeats.

Shattering glass alerts us that someone is trying to get in my back door, and I gasp.

"Stay behind me," Nixon instructs. I quickly move so he is in front of me, blocking anything from being able to get to me. "Whoever you are, I would advise you to leave now. I have a fully loaded pistol, and

I'm not afraid to shoot," he shouts, unholstering his gun and aiming it toward the back door.

Faint curses ring out before they disappear, but Nixon doesn't move.

"Call nine-one-one," he instructs, but my phone is too far away to reach.

"I left my phone on the couch," I whisper.

"Mine is in my left front pocket. Pull it out and call."

As I reach into his pocket, I realize how close we are. I take a sharp inhale, filling my nose with the scent of musk and something woodsy. *Holy shit, that's an amazing cologne scent.*

"Get the phone, Dante," Nixon growls out, pulling me out of my thoughts. I slide the device out of his pocket and dial 9-1-1.

After I relay the information, I stand still behind the giant of a man in front of me, trying to even my breathing. Not only am I scared shitless that someone tried to break into my house, but I'm also extremely turned on at how close I am to Nixon.

"The police are pulling into your driveway now," the dispatcher informs us, and we end the call.

Nixon escorts the officers inside and encourages me to sit on the couch again, then heads to check why the power went out. After he leaves, everything goes by in a bit of a blur. I give a report to the police officers, but the entire time, I feel like I'm not in my body.

Before I know it, Nixon is packing a bag for me and driving us to a hotel. Apparently, he always keeps an overnight bag in his car, just in case, so we don't have to stop at his house.

While we drive, he explains that some sort of power line was cut and will have to be fixed tomorrow. So tonight, I'm being forced to share a suite with a man I shouldn't be letting get closer to me. Yet I can't stop it.

After we are checked in, Nixon halls our bags to the room while I follow along, still feeling like this is a dream. *Why the hell did someone try to break into my place?* The moment a bed is in sight, I collapse onto it. I'm exhausted to the bone, yet my brain won't shut off.

"Do you need anything?" Nixon asks, leaning against the doorframe of my room for the night.

"Did the cameras pick up anything?" I ask instead of answering his question because honestly, I don't know what I need right now.

"Nope. Whoever this was knew all about your security system, which means they either scoped out your place or somehow had inside knowledge. I'm leaning toward the latter."

That causes me to jolt upright. "How the fuck would they have inside knowledge?"

"That's what we're trying to figure out. If someone were scoping out your place, I would have known."

I chew on the corner of my thumb.

Who would betray me?

"You shouldn't do that," Nixon scolds me.

I roll my eyes. "Bite me. I'm nervous. Someone tried to break into my house tonight. Or did you forget?" I snap, standing and making my way toward him. "Maybe it is one of your guys who is the insider."

Nixon's nostrils flair. "Not possible," he states with a growl, tightening his stance.

"How is it not possible? Are you that fucking perfect?"

"I'm not perfect, but I know everyone who works for me. It wasn't my team."

I roll my eyes again, loving the way it makes Nixon's teeth grind. One way to get my mind off the fact that someone broke my trust is by getting under the beast's skin. It's a good way to pass the time.

"Well, if it wasn't your team, who was it?"

"I don't know yet, but I *will* find out," he assures me.

"You keep saying things like that, but you've yet to prove yourself. Maybe I should hire a new team." I shrug, but as I turn to walk away, Nixon grabs my wrist.

A jolt of electricity shoots through my veins, and I bite my lip to stop the moan that wants to escape. A simple touch should *not* turn me on as much as it is.

"I get that you're scared, but stop being a brat for once," Nixon growls out.

I take a deep inhale before staring directly into his perfect baby blues. "Make me," I push, knowing exactly what I'm doing.

How much more do I have to press to make him break?

Nixon's eyes darken, and the grip on my wrist tightens. He's so close to snapping and punishing me. That's exactly what I want. What I need.

"Or are you a chickenshit?" I goad, making his jaw tick.

A deep guttural growl escapes him, and he licks his lips as he decides what he's going to do. All I know is I won't stop it. I want whatever he's going to give me, even if it will be a mistake at the end of the night.

I want Nixon Hunter, and by the look in his eyes right now, he wants me too.

Chapter 8

Nixon

WITH PENT-UP FRUSTRATION, I fling Dante onto the bed he was lying on a moment ago and pin his hands above his head, pressing my heavy body against his.

"Is this what you want?" I fume.

My lips are so close to his that with the slightest tilt of my head, I could claim his mouth, and everything inside of me is screaming to do exactly that, but I don't.

The smirk spreading across Dante's lips eggs me on even more. This is dangerous. I'm normally under complete control, but this man has my resolve slipping.

And it's terrifying.

"That all you got?" he challenges with a lifted brow.

I grind my molars and stand quickly. Dante pouts as an evil grin spreads across my lips.

"Get naked *now*," I command, and his pout fades, turning into an O of surprise, but he doesn't move to do as he's told. "I'm going to get what I want tonight, Dante," I say, crossing my arms over my chest. "You choose how you want it to end. If you want to come, you better get naked."

He stares at me for a second, obviously contemplating what he wants. After a few deep breaths, he sits up and pulls off his shirt.

"Good boy," I praise him, and his breath hitches as he stands.

There are a million things we should be doing *before* we take it to this level, but we both need this right now. Stopping isn't an option for either of us.

Once his pants are on the floor, he pauses, staring at his feet.

"Boxers too," I instruct, moving to sit on the bed.

Slowly, he pushes his underwear down and turns toward me, his giant cock proudly sticking out directly at me.

I take a moment to soak him in.

Dante isn't short at six feet, but I'm a good head taller than him at six-foot-eight. Where I'm broad and furry, Dante is slim and completely hair free. He's got washboard abs and a V that makes women weak at their knees. They just don't know he bats for the same team they do. His skin is creamy. *Fucking perfect.* I can't wait to turn the globes of his apple-shaped ass the brightest shade of red.

He'll have trouble walking tomorrow if he lets me go as far as I want to, but he'll love it. I can tell already.

He's staring at me as he pushes his hair out of his hazel eyes and licks his lips, lust and curiosity written all over his face. I wonder if he's done this before.

"What now?" he asks, without the attitude he typically harbors. In its place is a breathy impatience.

"Get over my knees," I instruct, and he doesn't disappoint. His breath hitches, doing as he's told. "See, it's not hard to listen."

He doesn't say anything, but I'm sure he's biting his tongue to stop a snappy comeback.

"Do you have a safe word?" I inquire as I rub his ass firmly but gently.

"No. I've never done anything like this before," Dante admits.

I should stop this now. He's a newbie. I could push him too far, and the last thing I want is to ever hurt anyone.

"Are you okay with this?" I check, and he nods. I squeeze my eyes shut and take a deep, cleansing breath. "I need your words," I grit out.

"I want this," he responds. "Please don't stop." His plea is all it takes to make me give in.

I fill my lungs deeply before exhaling slowly. "I'm going to give you five spankings. You will count as I do it. If you stop counting, I will start again. If it gets too much, you need to use a safe word. Tonight, we'll use the traffic light system. Green is good. Yellow means slow down, and red is stop. If you use red, everything stops. I'll still take care of you, but there won't be any sex, do you understand?"

He nods, and I huff out a breath of air.

"Sorry. Yes, I understand."

"This is going to hurt, but it will also feel really fucking good. You are not allowed to come until I tell you."

"Yes, Sir," he responds, and his words have my cock pushing so firmly against the restraint of my clothes I damn near come in my pants.

"Are you ready?"

He turns his head to look at me. "Yes, Sir," he says again, and I nod, unable to form words right now.

Lifting my hand, I bring it down firmly on his round white ass.

"Fuck," he cries out, and I click my tongue.

"Count, no other words," I remind him.

"One," he pants out as I rub out the sting of the slap.

Lifting my hand again, I smack the other cheek.

"Two," he cries out, his breathing becoming more labored from the two spankings.

If this wasn't his first time, the number would be much higher for the way he's been pushing my buttons, but we haven't gone over limits yet, and I'm not about to turn into a red flag of a Dom here. Kink requires respect, and I refuse to start this on an even more unbalanced standing than we already are. As it is, I'm breaking my own rule of not having an in-depth conversation first.

I pick up the speed of the spankings to get it over with so I can reward him for doing such a good job. Honestly, I'm surprised he isn't fighting me harder, but I'm glad he isn't, at least for tonight. If this continues, I would love for a night where he fights. My cock pushes against my clothes again, also loving the idea.

"Three, four, shiiit," he calls out as I spank him fast and hard.

"You were doing so good. Mmm," I hum, rubbing out the sting as I admire the cherry-red color of his firm ass. "Since this is your first time, I am going to give you a pass this once, but this last one is going to pack a bite." I bring back my hand and put a bit more force into it as I deliver the fifth and final spanking.

Dante's breath catches in his throat, but he manages to grit out, "Five, Sir."

"Good boy," I praise before pulling him off my lap and laying him on the bed.

Moving between his legs, I drop to my knees and run my tongue up the length of his erection, lapping up the precum when I get to the tip.

"Jesus." He gasps.

"You were such a good boy," I praise him again, wanting to reassure him. Then a hint of something I haven't seen in his eyes before appears. It's almost like insecurity. *Has he never been praised before?* "I'm going to suck your cock now. You can come when you need to," I say and dive in, swallowing him down my throat.

"Fuck." His moans and curses fill the room as I blow him like my life depends on it, showing off the fact that I don't have a gag reflex.

"I'm not going to last," he tells me, but I don't stop.

Instead, I pick up speed, humming a little around the base of his cock, relishing in the salty taste of his precum. That's when he blows, and I swallow every last drop like the greedy fucker I am.

His breathing is heavy as I release him from my mouth, letting him rest as I stand. "I'll be right back." I go grab a glass of water, a chocolate bar I keep in my bag, just in case, and some cream to soothe his tender ass.

"Roll onto your stomach," I instruct when I return, placing the water and chocolate on the nightstand.

He doesn't fight me, and there is even a small smile on his lips as I rub the lotion onto his still-red cheeks.

"Can I hold you?" I ask, pulling the blankets back and encouraging him to climb in.

"I'd like that," he whispers, and I get in beside him.

As soon as I'm positioned, he cuddles into my side. He fits fucking perfectly in my arms, and I'm not sure what I should do with that information.

My heart does a couple of flips, but I shut it down. This isn't anything special. I've had a million nights like this. I'm just taking care of a sub who I played with, nothing more.

"Sit up for a minute. You need to drink some water. I also have a chocolate bar for you."

"Thank you," he replies as we adjust to a sitting position, staying close, and he rests his head on my shoulder.

He sips the water, then takes a bite of the chocolate when I hold it to his lips.

"Tomorrow, we are going to talk about this," I state firmly. He nods, but a yawn slips past his lips.

"Will you stay with me?" he requests with sleepy eyes.

There is no way I could tell him no, even if I wanted to. "Of course, just let me take my clothes off."

I slip out of bed and strip to my boxers. My cock tents the material, and Dante's eyes zero in on it.

"Not tonight, Brat. We have a lot we need to discuss first," I tell him.

The pout he offers me makes me chuckle, but I'm not caving on that. I already crossed a line I shouldn't have. No way am I fucking him until we have a deep conversation and set up boundaries.

The moment I'm in bed again, Dante clings to me. It makes me smile for a second before I correct my face. I shouldn't be this fucking happy with him in my arms. Even if we continue something kinky, this isn't a relationship. Dante isn't my boyfriend. Best if we both understand and accept that as soon as possible.

But as Dante's lips press into my chest for a gentle kiss, it's obvious I'm fucked.

As I wake to the phone ringing by my head, I'm a sweaty mess.

"Shh," a deep murmuring comes from my chest while I blink my eyes open.

Shit, I forgot I fell asleep with Dante last night.

I reach out for the phone and sigh when I see it's Denver calling.

"What?" I bark out as quietly as possible.

He laughs. "Power's back on at Dante's place. Did you not sleep well?"

"Something like that," I murmur. "Can you and Bennett head over there and make sure everything is okay?"

"Yup, that was already part of the plan. We also have the repair guy lined up to meet us there in about thirty minutes. I'll keep you updated."

"Thanks," I reply and end the call.

I carefully move to get out of bed, but Dante snuggles in deeper.

"Don't go," he whimpers.

I'm pretty sure he's still asleep, but for the life of me, I can't make myself move. Not when he begs like that. Asleep or not.

Sighing, I give in and cuddle under the blankets, holding him for a while.

It's my stomach that wakes me the second time. Thankfully, I'm able to escape without a pouty boy demanding I stay.

Once I'm in the suite's main living room, I call for breakfast, then make my way to the bathroom to get ready for the day. After I'm dressed, the food arrives, and I set it on the table and sit to do a few tasks on my phone.

"Is that bacon I smell?" Dante asks a little while later, yawning widely and stretching his arms to the roof.

I set down my phone, staring at him, my heart racing a little at the perfect sight of him. He put on a pair of boxers, but they aren't hiding much. Besides, I've already seen him naked and have an excellent memory.

"Yup, there is a little bit of everything. I wasn't sure what you wanted," I say with a shrug.

"Is there coffee?" he inquires with narrowed eyes, and I laugh.

"Obviously. I've worked for you long enough to know you'll bite anyone's head off if you aren't sufficiently caffeinated."

He nods and sits beside me, reaching for the carafe.

"What's the plan for today?" he asks, then plops a piece of bacon in his mouth. Of course, I can't help but watch.

He licks his lips to catch the little drip of grease, and my cock thickens. *Shit, I should have rubbed one out in the shower this morning.* It's going to be a long-ass day without having any sort of release. Maybe that's why I'm getting so turned on by him simply eating a piece of bacon.

"I need to grab a few things from my office. I should also stop at my place to pack a better bag, but other than that, there isn't much on the agenda. By the time we get to your house, everything will be fixed and in working order."

"Why do you need to pack again?" he pries with his brows pulled together, obviously confused. *How is that look hot on him? Yep, I should have rubbed one out this morning.*

"Because you have a new roommate for the time being," I tease, unable to hide my smirk.

His face turns angry. "Fuck no," he growls out.

"It's not up for debate, Dante. It's no longer safe for you to stay at your house alone."

He glares at me but doesn't argue further. But, of course, it wouldn't matter even if he did. It's too risky now.

"I also don't want you to tell *anyone* that I'm staying with you. I'll park my SUV in the garage at night. We have no clue who the insider is, but at this point, we can't trust anybody."

"Not even Anna?" He gasps, and I hate the pained look in his eyes at the idea of keeping his best friend in the dark.

I shake my head slowly, even though I hate keeping her in the dark. "I don't think it's her, but we aren't taking any chances here. Your safety is my number one priority."

He nibbles on his lip but nods.

"Okay, with that sorted out, we need to talk about last night," I say as Dante takes a bite of a strawberry. "How are you feeling today?"

"Sore," he murmurs, but there is a smirk on his lips.

"Do you regret what we did?"

"No. I needed it. It felt really good."

The corners of my lips turn up at his admission, and my chest fills with pride. "Good. I don't normally do *anything* with a person before going over limits and boundaries and having a deep conversation. So I wanted to apologize for not doing that with you."

"You don't have any reason to apologize. I pushed your buttons. I was aware of what I was doing, even if it was my first time doing kinky things. Can we still have that conversation?"

I blink at him, shocked he wants to continue this.

"Do you think it's the best idea to have a relationship with your babysitter?" I tease, but that fire behind his eyes doesn't fade.

"I mean, if you're not up to it, I understand. You are old, after all." He cocks his head to the side with a mischievous smirk on his lips and a shrug of his shoulders.

"You must love having a sore ass," I retort, and his smile grows, but he keeps quiet. "I'll print some stuff off at my office. We can have a conversation this afternoon."

He squirms in his chair and nods. "Perfect."

I guess we are doing this.

I'm so fucked.

Chapter 9

Dante

WHEN WE GET TO my house, I'm surprised by what I see. Everything is exactly how it was before the incident. The back door is fixed, all the broken glass is cleaned up, and nothing is out of the ordinary. It's almost like something terrifying didn't take place last night.

But it did.

My heart races as I stare at the door. I want to run away, but my feet refuse to move as something squeezes my chest tightly, making it hard to breathe.

"Are you okay?" Nixon asks when I don't move for a few moments, his tone gentle.

I remain still, unable to find the words. I'm *not* okay, but I don't know how to tell him that. Do I admit I don't feel safe here anymore? No, I can't do that. We don't have that kind of relationship, and I'm not sure I want to develop one, either. I want to fuck, mess around, and unearth my kinky side, but I don't want to catch feelings. The only way to do that is to create emotional distance.

I take a slow, deep breath before turning on my heels.

"I'm fine," I say, brushing past Nixon.

"I don't like it when you lie to me," Nixon grumbles, following me.

"Is it safe for us to hang outside? The sun is shining. I'd like to work on my tan," I say, completely bypassing Nixon's remark.

"It should be fine. Your pool area is secluded enough. I'll get a notification if anyone steps foot on the property."

I nod and make my way to my room.

As soon as I'm inside, I shut the door behind me, lean against it, close my eyes, and take a few deep breaths. I need to get my shit together. Nixon can't know how much I'm affected by everything that's going on because he is the type of guy who will pry while trying to get me to open up.

I can't let him in.

It isn't safe.

I need to build my wall again and do as I've always done—keep people at arm's length. Our relationship will be purely physical, nothing more.

I take another calming breath, push off the door, and go to my dresser, picking out a pair of navy-blue swim trunks. After I'm changed, I grab a pair of black aviators and head outside, where Nixon is already waiting.

How is he not dying of heat stroke in his black T-shirt? Even if he did change into a pair of shorts, which are also black, there is no way he's cool right now.

"What all did you print off?" I ask, eyeing the shit ton of papers in front of him, my palms sweating.

"I printed off a few limits lists I want us to go over together," he states. "I know this is new to you, but a lot of new partners start out with these checklists. It helps them get to know each other better and to feel like they can express their boundaries and limits without judgment."

He lifts his sunglasses to rest on top of his head, and his baby blues stare intently into my eyes. *Why does that always make it hard for me to breathe?* Yet, at the same time, it almost eases some of the nerves that suddenly appeared.

"We can pause at any time to talk about anything. So don't be afraid to speak up. This is all about us getting to know each other and making sure we are comfortable with the same things. I want to know what you want from this dynamic and what you expect from me. I'll also have rules and expectations for you. After, we'll go over safe words and aftercare. Do you have any questions so far?"

I shake my head, and my stomach wobbles a little—not from nerves but excitement.

"Hand me a list," I say eagerly, reaching out while trying to appear patient. But by the smirk on Nixon's face as he places the papers and a pen in my hand, I'd say I failed.

"I'm surprised you aren't making some sort of comment about the list," Nixon mutters as I give the first page a quick read.

"I mean, it does seem kind of boring, but I like the idea that it's going to keep us both safe."

"That's the idea. It lets us both know what we are and aren't comfortable with. There are a bunch of different types of limit check sheets out there, but I like this one."

I look over the top of the list and fill it out easily.

Am I a Dom, submissive, or Switch? Sub.

Experience Level? Total newbie isn't an answer, so I check beginner.

Sexual Orientation? Ugh, such boring responses. Why isn't queer as fuck an answer? I put my mark next to gay because, obviously, I'm not straight.

How do I prefer this relationship?

My eyes hover over the word polyamorous, and a rare feeling of jealousy creeps over my body. Without hesitation, I put a check next to monogamous and glanced at Nixon. *Would I be able to share him if he asked me to? Fuck, I don't know.*

How do I prefer to dress during a scene? Denim sounds like it would chafe. Gothic isn't my thing. Lace is actually intriguing. Latex or rubber isn't too appealing to me. Leather is a maybe. I write out my thoughts since there is a place to put other ideas.

"Can we try different styles of dress for scenes?" I ask, earning a smile from Nixon.

"Absolutely. I'm not going to lie, I prefer you naked, but you'd also be sexy as fuck in lace."

Heat creeps up my cheeks, and I'm sure I'm a bright shade of red as I finish the last part of the first page, marking no next to any health conditions or limitations. I'm not normally one to blush at compliments, but the way Nixon speaks has me feeling all warm and gooey inside.

"Now we are getting to the fun part," Nixon notes. "Next to each limit are three boxes for experience. Never means you have never done something. Tried means you've done it once or twice but not enough to judge fully. Versed means you are confident in your opinion of it at this time. Then you'll rate that on a scale of zero to five. Zero means you *hate* it. One is begrudgingly accepted. Two, neutral negative. Three, neutral positive. Four is something you actively like, and five is something you *love*."

It all sounds pretty straight forward.

"Next, you'll want to rate your comfort level of doing something in the future. The options are hard, soft, curious, enjoy, and fav. Hard means something you are absolutely *not* wanting to participate in, no matter what. Soft is something you are not usually interested in but would be willing to try in the right circumstance, but extensive conversation would have to be had. Curious is something you want to explore but would want to discuss prior to. Enjoy is something that is fair game, and fav is something you love and would want to be included often..."

He pauses, glancing into my eyes intently to check in. I offer him a small grin and a tilt of my head for him to continue.

"After that, there are columns for fetish and forced. Fetish is something you absolutely *need*. Something you wouldn't feel complete without in this dynamic. Forced is something you feel you want or need to be *forced* to do to enjoy. Limits can change over time, so we are always able to come back to these." I nod. "Any questions?"

"Nope. I think it's all straightforward."

He stares into my eyes, almost like he's trying to figure out if I'm lying. As soon as he's done checking in on me, we start.

As we make our way through the list, I notice I'm getting extremely turned-on, even when I come across activities that are hard limits for me. We occasionally stop so I can ask questions, but for the most part, we work in comfortable silence. My whole body lights up when we get to impact play and spanking.

Impact play is something I know I'll enjoy, but spanking is a fetish. I don't want to not have that in my life. The way my entire body released last night when he spanked me sent me to fucking heaven. It was glorious and like everything was set right.

By the time we finish the list, my cock is throbbing, wanting so badly to be touched, but I'm not sure if that will get me in trouble or not. I mean, we haven't finished the contract yet, and honestly, trouble sounds like a good time, but for whatever reason, I leave my erection alone.

"Can we switch lists for a minute?" Nixon asks, and I nod, handing him my papers as I accept his.

We go over the lists in silence, and I smile when I see we are compatible. Thankfully, Nixon also checked monogamous, and I no longer have to figure out if I'm capable of sharing. Heat creeps up my body when I see he's into tying people up because that's something I want to try. A lot. Nothing he has as *musts* are a no-go for me, and the same for him. None of his hard limits are a must for me.

"I know you're new to all of this, but I want to know what you really want. How do you want me to make you feel? What are you expecting from this relationship?" Nixon inquires after he finishes reading my list.

"I don't want you to be my boyfriend," I start, making the corners of his lips tick. "I want this to be mostly physical. Obviously, I'm expecting some emotions to get involved in certain aspects, but for the most part, I'm looking for you to control me in the bedroom, and that's it."

"I'm a control freak. Can some of that control bleed into life beyond the bedroom? I'm not asking to be your boyfriend, but in order for me to feel fulfilled in this, I want more than just sex."

I let the words roll around in my head for a minute and then nod.

"I don't think I *hate* that. What I was mainly getting at is a deep emotional connection. I'm not looking for you to want to get into my soul."

Nixon nods. "I can respect that. What else do you want?"

"I'm not one hundred percent sure. Is it possible for us to figure that out as we go? I know for sure I like giving up control in the bedroom, but I also like pushing your buttons. I like when you spank me because it causes this amazing release. Other than that, I'm not too sure what I need just yet."

Nixon smiles. "Everything is always up for discussion. Lots of dynamics start out with basic rules and evolve over time."

"What about you? What do you need?" I ask, and his eyes blaze with something almost like pride.

"I obviously like control, but one of my biggest things is caring for the person I'm with. That's why aftercare is always a must for me. I need it as much as you do."

"I liked you holding me last night," I admit.

"I liked it far more than I think I should have," he mumbles, and I laugh.

"What else?" I inquire, wanting to learn more about him and what he wants from this dynamic. So far, we are on the same page, and I hope it stays that way.

"I'm a big fan of rules, but we can create those as this grows, as we get to know each other better and find out what we both need and want."

I mull over his words. How do I *really* feel about rules? I guess it would depend on what they are.

"Can you explain the rules to me a little better? Are they a *must*-do? How does it work?"

"Some are a must. Others, you *could* choose to break them, but there would be consequences."

My mind drifts to the idea of more spankings and possibly more impact play, and my entire body lights up.

"Like what?"

"Spankings are more of funishments and not punishments, Brat," he states, and I pout. "Like if you roll your eyes or sass back, those would result in spankings. But say I asked you to eat three meals a day, and you only ate two. Maybe that night I would edge you all night long but not let you come."

I'm not sure how I feel about that, and I must pull a face because Nixon grabs my hand and squeezes it.

"But everything is negotiable. I won't ever do anything you aren't comfortable with. We'll agree on what works best for both of us. If we hit a stalemate, then we go our separate ways."

I nibble on my lip but nod after mulling it over for a moment. "Okay. That makes sense to me."

"How do you feel about honorifics?" he asks, bringing it back to a subject that's more fun.

"I liked calling you Sir last night," I reply.

"It sounded good coming from your lips. That's my preferred honorific. Are you okay with referring to me that way when we are alone?"

"I don't see why not."

"What do you want to be called?" he inquires, and I let myself think about it before blurting anything out.

"I like it when you call me Brat, but I don't think that suits every situation. What about Treasure?"

Nixon studies me briefly before responding. "Why that?"

I shrug and chew on my lower lip. "I used to dream about being special and treasured by someone. Heaven knows my parents never treated me that way. So Treasure just feels right to me."

Nixon's face softens, and he nods with a bright smile. "It's perfect," he whispers, staring intently into my eyes. "Okay, onto aftercare. For now, we can come back to the rules later." I nod and wait for him to continue. "How do you want to be cared for after a scene?"

"I really liked the way you held me and fed me chocolate," I tell him. "My favorite chocolate bar is a KitKat, though. Could we make that a thing?"

"Absolutely, I always want you to have your favorites. Do you like stuffed animals or have a special blanket you would like to cuddle with?"

I shake my head, but a stuffed animal sounds nice. "I don't have any, but those giant stuffies at the store always catch my eye. I've just never let myself buy one before."

He writes something down on his paper, and I'm dying to know what it is.

"I also think I will need you to sleep with me after every scene," I say as he sets his pen down, but something feels off. The idea of sleeping alone, with everything that's happening right now, makes me sick to my stomach. "Actually, since you're living here for the time being, could we sleep together *every* night? It would make me feel safer."

Nixon's jaw goes tight before he responds, and I wonder if he doesn't like the suggestion.

"We can make that a part of our agreement. Every night while I'm living here, we sleep in the same bed."

I grin as a rush of relief washes through my body. "That sounds perfect. My love language is physical touch," I add.

"I kind of figured with how much you clung to me last night," he remarks with a smirk.

"What is your love language?" I ask, wanting to make sure I am giving as much as I'm taking.

"Physical touch and words of affirmation."

"Perfect. I'll make sure to keep that in mind. So you aren't into degradation, then?" I check, and he shakes his head.

"If the person I'm with *really* needs it, I'll try, but I don't even like being the one degrading someone."

"Good thing that isn't my kink," I tease.

"No, you just like a sore ass to go with that smart mouth."

I laugh. *He isn't wrong.*

"Now, on to safe words. Do you have a preference?" Nixon inquires.

"I think I like the traffic light system. Having to remember a specific word doesn't sound appealing to me."

"Completely fine. Use them when you need them. That's why they are there. You'll never get punished for using your safe word."

I smile, and when my stomach grumbles, I realize it's later in the day than I thought it was.

"Are you hungry?" he asks, and I nod.

"I guess we skipped lunch."

"What would you like for dinner?" he asks, pulling out his phone.

"What, you're not cooking for me?" I joke, and he narrows his eyes at me.

"It's been a long day. I think takeout will be okay for one night," he retorts.

"Good thing I'm easy," I reply with a wink.

He chuckles and shakes his head.

"Are you on a specific diet for this role?" he checks, keeping his eyes on his phone.

"Not this time. I just have to stay in general shape. I'm kind of lucky I can still eat whatever I want as long as I work out at least six days a week. Speaking of, once we're done ordering our food, I'm gonna swim some laps for a bit."

"Sounds good. I like to watch," Nixon replies with a waggle of his brows, sending a jolt straight to my cock.

"What's your favorite restaurant?"

I tell him about a sandwich shop I found a few years ago that makes the absolute best food and has a delivery system. As soon as our order is placed, I stand and stretch before strutting over to the water, making sure to put a little extra swing in my hips so his eyes are drawn to my ass. I mean, if you can't flaunt your *assets,* what good is it being in shape like this?

As I step into the water, I realize I'm *really* happy with Nixon here, but I shouldn't be. Instead, I should be pissed he's taking up space in my sanctuary.

The way I react to Nixon terrifies me, but what do I do about it?

Chapter 10

Nixon

IT DOESN'T TAKE LONG for the food to arrive. My mouth waters from the aroma that wafts out of the bag as I carry it into the house.

How the hell do sandwiches smell that good?

My stomach rumbles. Apparently, I was hungrier than I thought. *Man, I can't wait to devour these bad boys.*

After stopping at the refrigerator to grab some water, I bring the food and drinks to the back patio and wait for Dante to join me. He's toweling off, and naturally, I keep a close eye on him. Of course, I could lie to myself and say it's because it is my job, but what's the point? It's obviously more than that with him.

"I'm fucking starving," Dante complains as he plops down in a chair at the table.

"Good thing I ordered extra. It's my fault for skipping lunch. I promise I won't let that happen again."

"I often skip meals. It's not a big deal. I just make up for it at the next one," Dante shares nonchalantly, but that doesn't sit right with me.

"That's going to stop. It's not healthy for you. Especially someone who works out as often as you do. You need three meals a day, plus snacks." He rolls his eyes. "Should I start tallying your eye rolls now?"

He gasps, and his eyebrows shoot up. "What?"

"I'm thinking it would be fun to tally all your eye rolls and give you daily spankings," I state. "If you're still a good boy at the end of the day, you'll get rewarded, but if you miss your meals, it will be spankings only, no orgasms. What do you think?"

He glares at me before taking a bite of his sandwich. Watching his mouth move and the way his tongue sticks out to clean his lips does something to me. *How is that turning me on right now? Have I been this infatuated with others in the past?* I don't think so, but I don't want to dwell on this new information, so I push it aside.

"That sounds fine," he grumbles, but he's squirming in his seat at the thought, so I know he likes it.

We sit in peaceful silence as we eat. Being with Dante isn't awkward or uncomfortable—quite the opposite, actually. I'm not a person who has the need to fill all silence with pointless chatter, and I'm glad he's the same.

"Are things changing for work tomorrow?" Dante asks after finishing his first sandwich.

"I want to keep everything as close to our normal as possible. I'd rather not clue whoever the insider is in. Besides, the chances of them wanting to attack you at work are slim to none. If they try something stupid like that, I'm confident in my abilities to protect you. They won't get close enough to even breathe on you, let alone *touch* you," I assure him.

"I keep asking myself, why me? What have I ever done to someone to make them want to hurt me? And why would someone I let close to me want to help them? It just doesn't make sense. I'm not a bad guy."

I reach across the table and place my hand on his, giving it a gentle squeeze. His eyes meet mine while I try to find the right words for him, having this overwhelming need to make it better for him. "I wish I had answers for you, but I don't. I do have an idea to get your mind off everything, though." My cock takes notice of the way Dante's eyes light up. But my idea isn't of the sexy variety, even though I'm sure that's where the sexy actor's mind has gone.

"What's that?" He leans toward me, his voice dripping with sexual need.

"*Mario Party* on your Nintendo Switch," I tell him with a cheeky grin, laughing when he grumbles under his breath at what an ass I am.

Begrudgingly, he gives in, and it's not until we have played three *Mario Party* rounds and watched two movies that I realize what time it is.

"Bedtime, Treasure," I instruct.

"But I'm not tired," he whines, and my hand twitches, wanting to turn that ass red.

I have to bite my tongue to stop the smile from spreading. There's something about a man who exudes confidence and finesse to the public eye but is pouting for me that turns me on. But it also makes me proud he's letting part of his wall down enough around me to do it.

"You have to get up early tomorrow, so you're going to bed," I state, but he doesn't move when I stand. Instead, he crosses his arms over his chest and glares at me. I run my tongue along my teeth, and the corners of my lips turn up into an evil grin. "If you get up now and go to your room, I'll let you come after your spankings. You've been a good boy today. I really want to reward you." The words almost come out in a purr, and I chuckle as Dante bolts past me. "Get naked and wait by the bed on your knees," I holler after him.

I take my time cleaning up the entertainment room before making my way to Dante's room—the room we'll be sharing while I'm staying here.

When Dante first suggested that, my knee-jerk reaction was to say no. I've never done that with a sub before. Honestly, I've never lived with a partner, which might be weird, considering I'm in my forties, but work has always been my life. Before I started Hunter Security, my all was for the Army. I wasn't a boyfriend kind of guy. Everyone I have ever been with has always been casual, so this is all new territory for me.

But I couldn't tell Dante no, especially with how vulnerable and scared he looked when we first arrived at his house after the break-in. I'm certain he doesn't feel safe here anymore. But I'll gladly do it if I can calm some of those nerves by sleeping with him at night.

As I walk into the bedroom, I'm pleasantly surprised to find Dante in the position I requested. "Such a good boy," I praise, reaching behind my neck to pull off my shirt.

"Will you fuck me tonight?" he requests with pleading eyes as I walk around the bed to place my gun in the side table drawer.

"Is that what you want?" I ask, moving back to stand in front of him.

I unbuckle my belt, letting my eyes roam over his body. His cock is sticking out proudly with a bit of precum already beading at the tip. Clearly, my boy is a leaker, and I love it.

"Yes," Dante responds to my question. "I really want you to fuck me."

I nod while unbuttoning my shorts, pushing them and my boxers to the floor before slowly stepping out. "How do you want it?" I inquire, stroking my cock and taking note of the way Dante's eyes zero in on it.

"Hard, please, Sir," he begs, bringing a smile to my face as I strut over to the bed and sit in front of where Dante is kneeling.

I gently grip his chin, tilting his face toward mine and staring into his gorgeous eyes. There is a mix of the fire I've grown to enjoy, lust, and a tiny bit of insecurity, reminding me I need to make sure this is an amazing experience for him. "First, I want you to suck my cock," I instruct. "Then I will give you your three spankings. After, I will fuck your brains out."

His pupils dilate more, almost as if he is high. It turns me on more than it should. Feelings like this are easy to get addicted to, and Dante is the last man on Earth I should fall for. He's so deep in the closet with no signs of wanting to come out anytime soon. He can't give me what I want long term.

I blow out a breath, getting my head in the game again. Now isn't the time to succumb to those thoughts. With a firm grip on my cock, I use my other hand, still on Dante's chin, to pull him toward me.

"Open, Treasure," I demand, loving the way he quickly obeys, sticking his out tongue to lick the tip of my dick. "Fuck." I gasp, moving my hand to the back of his head. I push him down on my throbbing erection, and he groans. The vibration sends a shutter of heat down my spine.

He's a greedy little cock slut as he slurps and bobs up and down. Every time he gags, I wonder if I'm going to blow. The way his throat constricts around my cock is almost too much to handle, but I can't help but push him down a little further. Again, he gags, followed by a cough with saliva and precum dripping from the corners of his mouth.

Releasing my hold, I let him have his way for a little while, leaning back on my elbows and watching him. His eyes are watery from gagging, and his lips are swollen from how well he's sucking. The sight of him swallowing me down has me impatient. So I sit up, guide his head down one more time, and hold, relishing in the feeling. Then, when he moans around my shaft, I place my hands on his face, slowly pulling him off. And like the cock slut he is, he hollows his cheeks all the way up, and my breath shudders as I try not to come.

"Such a good boy," I tell him as I help him stand and guide him to bend over my knees. "Are you ready to count?"

He slowly tilts his head toward me. "Yes, Sir," he replies, smiling before letting his head hang again.

The three spankings go by quickly, and before I know it, I'm tossing Dante onto the bed, pointing my finger at him. "Stay," I command. "I have to get the lube and condoms because I'm a dumb ass and left them in my bag in the kitchen."

He chuckles as I head to the kitchen to grab my bags, quickly looking around out of habit. Thankfully, nothing is out of the ordinary, and I can rush back to the sexy boy waiting for me.

"What took you so long?" Dante asks as I drop my bags by the bedroom door. He's braced on one elbow with his free hand lazily stroking his cock.

I raise a brow at him. "Did I say you could touch?"

He doesn't stop. "You didn't say I *couldn't* touch," he retorts, the sass in his tone not going unnoticed.

"Well, I'm saying it now. Stop touching your cock, or I'm not fucking you tonight," I inform Dante, and he pouts but slowly removes his hand.

Grabbing a condom and the bottle of lube, I stride over to the bed and set the supplies on the nightstand. Once my hands are free, I climb onto the bed and straddle Dante, bringing my lips close to his but not kissing him yet. Instead, I reach between us and grab his cock firmly, staring intently into his eyes. "This is mine while we are together. You will ask before touching from now on. Do you understand?" I growl, and Dante pants beneath me.

"Yes, Sir," he answers breathlessly.

Needing to know what Dante's mouth tastes like, I let go of his cock, place both my hands on either side of his head, and *finally* do something I've been dreaming about for far too long. The moment my lips crash to his, Dante's back bows off the bed, and he moans into my mouth. Our cocks rub together, making me groan as he bucks his hips into me.

He tastes like perfection, like something I could see myself craving every day. Fuck, this boy is making me feel things I've never felt, and I wonder if I should call this off after tonight. Even as the thought filters through, I know I won't be able to do it. I guess I'll have to deal with the fallout when this ends.

Breaking away from his lips, I trail kisses to his neck, the salty chlorine from his pool clinging to his skin. "I so badly want to fucking mark you right now," I growl out, knowing I can't bite him or his director would be royally pissed.

"Mark me where they can't see," he suggests.

I pull away, studying his eyes. "Do you mean it?" I need verbal confirmation, not wanting to push his boundaries.

"Please," he begs, whimpering with need.

Kissing my way down his body, I nibble here and there, making sure not to leave marks until I get to his thighs.

"Do you have any naked scenes I need to be aware of?" I ask.

He laughs. "This is a kid's superhero movie. Pretty sure nudity is off the table."

I smile against his skin, kissing him gently and leisurely stroking his cock before I sink my teeth into his inner thigh.

"Yes," Dante cries out as I suck and bite, leaving my mark.

I'm not even sure why I had this deep desire to mark him, but it was like my soul wouldn't have been satisfied until it was done.

After I'm done, I grab the lube, pour a little onto my fingers, and push my index finger to Dante's puckered entrance. When I'm met with a little resistance as I try to push in, I lean forward and suck his cock, getting him to relax.

His body releases its tension, and I press my finger in, relishing in the moans and sighs of pleasure from his beautiful mouth. I pulse my finger in and out of his perfect ass, not sucking on his cock too much. I don't want him to come yet. I want to be inside him when that happens, but I *have* to stretch him. His channel is choking my finger so tight there is no way I could get my dick in without seriously hurting him.

"Breathe," I instruct, sliding in a second finger. He sucks in a shaky breath through his teeth before blowing it out, letting his body relax. "That's it. Let me stretch you good so I can fuck this gorgeous ass," I grit out. He smiles and throws his head back with a magnificent moan as I scissor my fingers.

It takes some time, but finally, he's relaxed enough to allow me to slip a third finger in. Then, after a few minutes of working him up, I'm sure he can take me.

"I feel so empty," Dante says after I pull my fingers out.

"You won't be for long," I promise, sliding the condom on and adding extra lube. "Get on your knees," I instruct firmly.

He eagerly moves into position, and I stand behind him, running my hand up and down his spine while I line myself up with his puckered entrance. "Are you ready?" I check in with him.

He peeks at me over his shoulder with a glorious blissed-out smirk.

"Please, Sir. Fuck me," he pleads, needy and wanting.

I don't want to keep this gorgeous boy waiting, so I push my hips forward, gently sinking into him. "Jesus." I moan as I fill him, loving the way his channel hugs me. "You feel so good," I praise him.

"Ungh," he responds, unable to form real words.

"Good?" I ask, and he nods. This time, I don't chastise him because I know I'm not going to be able to last, and I want him to come with me.

Once I'm fully seated inside him, I bend over and press a kiss between his shoulder blades, followed by a few nips. Dante groans deeply, clenching around me, and I gasp.

"You're so fucking perfect," I whisper.

He shakes his head, but no words leave his lips. I hate that he's feeling self-conscious. He should know and believe how amazing he is.

As soon as I'm certain he's grown accustomed to my size, I move, gripping his hips firmly but keeping my motions slow at first. Then I pick up my speed, ready to give us both what we want.

It doesn't take long for a tingle to form in the base of my spine as I pound into him, my fingers digging into his creamy skin, hopefully leaving more marks.

"Please, Sir, I need to come," he begs, and I'm happy he is as close as I am.

Leaning forward, I slip my hand around him to stroke his cock while I give him everything I have. Slapping of skin and moans of lust fill the room as I let go, fucking him as hard and as fast as I can.

After a few good strokes, Dante is crying out and releasing onto the bed. His ass squeezes me so tightly I swear I almost black out as my orgasm takes over, and I fill the condom.

I've never been bare with anyone, but an image of my load leaking out of his ass pops into my head. And I like the idea *a lot*.

After our breathing evens out and our hearts aren't beating so fast anymore, I slide out of him and rush to the bathroom to grab a washcloth and discard the condom. On the way back, I stop at my bag to get a KitKat bar and a bottle of water, then clean up the tired boy.

Lifting the blankets, I encourage Dante to get under before joining him. I lean against the headboard while he rests his head on my shoulder and lets me feed him a couple bites of chocolate.

As I bring the bottle of water to his lips and watch him drink, I can't help but think how different this feels from anyone I've ever been with.

Why the fuck did the universe think a closeted actor was the one for me?

Chapter 11

Dante

ONE OF MY FAVORITE things is becoming waking in Nixon's arms. That alone should make me want to push him away, but I can't. Simply being near him helps calm my nerves, and I need that right now. Maybe after everything settles, I'll figure out what to do about my addiction to him. That's all it is. It's not like he owns my heart or anything.

My phone buzzes next to me, alerting me to what woke me before the sun was even up. Normally, I would ignore it, but as I glance to see who could be calling at such an ungodly hour, I pick it up.

"Bitch, I miss you," I answer, and Anna giggles.

"I miss you too. Sorry I haven't called sooner. Life has been crazy here…" She pauses, then releases a sigh, and I wish I could hug her.

"It's all good. Life has been a little crazy for me too," I respond, trying to think of what I can actually tell her. Of course, there is no way Anna is the insider, but I want to respect Nixon's wishes.

"Tell me all about Paris," I redirect, trying to keep the focus off me.

"It's good," she answers, but her voice is dim. It's missing the normal over-the-top excited energy she usually holds, and I don't like it.

"What's wrong?" I plead, not missing the way she sucks in a breath.

"Brittany feels distant, and this gig isn't what I was expecting." She whimpers, and it breaks my heart.

"Oh, babe, I'm so sorry. Why do you think Brittany is being distant?"

"It's probably just the job, but something feels different," she murmurs, and I make a mental note to send Brittany a text message.

Anna isn't always the best at communicating, and I doubt Brittany knows anything is off. Brittany isn't the type of person to purposefully create distance, and she's typically excellent at dealing with Anna's mini freakouts, so I'm sure it won't be much to fix the problem.

"I'm sure it's nothing, sweetie, but I'm always here to talk. What about the job is wrong?"

"The hours are fucked." She groans. "They put in a clause in the contract I must not have read, stating they have the right to change working hours at any point during filming, so instead of being mostly day shifts, it's *all* been nights. It's like I'm a vampire, but I feel like a zombie."

I chuckle because I've had films like that before.

"If they keep you on night shifts, you'll get used to it," I assure her. "It's far worse to be switching back and forth constantly."

"I wasn't made for work like this," she complains, and I can imagine her pretending to faint or something. "A beautiful woman like me needs my beauty sleep."

"You'll get plenty after the filming is over."

I hear a voice in the background, and Anna sighs. "Food is here. I have to go. I promise I'll call again soon."

"Okay. Talk soon," I tell her, smiling, even though she can't see it. I'm hoping she can *hear* it. "And if you need *anything,* I'm here for you."

We end the call, and I set my phone on the nightstand again before cuddling up to Nixon, resting my head on his chest. His arms encircle me, invoking a calming sensation through my body. He must have woken sometime during the phone call.

"Want to work out with me?" I ask after a few heartbeats of silence.

"It's three in the morning," he grumbles.

"Once I'm awake, I can't fall back asleep," I admit. "You don't have to come, but that's where I'll be."

Lifting my hands, I stretch my body, then climb out of bed and grab a pair of workout shorts. As soon as I'm dressed, I head to the kitchen to fill a water bottle, aware of the footsteps behind me.

"How can you work out first thing yet hate mornings?" Nixon complains and then yawns. He lifts one arm to stretch while his other hand scratches his hairy stomach, and I hate that he also put on workout shorts.

"Honestly, the endorphins are almost as good as coffee." Nixon lifts a brow. "I said *almost*." I chuckle. "You can bet your ass I'll be having a giant cup the second we're done."

I fill a second water bottle, walk over to him, and pat his chest.

"Do you think I can out-bench you?" I challenge.

The smile spreading across his face is pure evil.

And I fucking love it.

"In your dreams, Brat."

I chuckle, walking past him to my gym.

"I'm stronger than I look," I call out over my shoulder.

"Want to bet on it?" he asks and pinches my ass, making me scream like a schoolgirl.

"Nah, I'm good," I respond, knowing full well there is no way I'll *actually* be able to out-bench him.

"Didn't take you for a chickenshit," Nixon goads.

I turn to glare at him. "I'm not afraid. I just don't want you to hurt yourself," I lie.

"Come on... we could make it interesting." He leans down, his lips so close to mine that his breath washes over my face.

"What do you have in mind?" I ask, my voice husky and my cock throbbing as it pushes my shorts out.

"You win, and I'll let you take charge tonight. Anything you say goes," Nixon states. My brows shoot up, filling me with intrigue. "But if I win, I get to do what I want."

Truth be told, that doesn't sound like a bad thing.

"You're on," I concede, walking to the bench press and loading the first set of weights before lying down. "But remember, I'm a lot younger than you. Don't push those old muscles too far."

Teasing Nixon is honestly my favorite thing right now. The way he grinds his molars makes my smile grow even wider as I lift the weights and do my first set.

"Come on, Old Man. Your turn," I say as I get up and wave my hand at the empty bench.

"I can't wait to punish you tonight," he grumbles, taking his place.

"That's only if you win," I remind him with a cheeky grin.

"I never lose."

It doesn't take me long to realize exactly how fucked I am.

Thankfully, Nixon is standing close as I press my last set, so he can help me lift the final weight off my chest. I'm panting like crazy, but there is still a smile on my face. I knew I would lose, but I gave it my all anyway.

"I'm surprised you got that high," Nixon states, and I narrow my eyes at him.

"How high can you bench?" I ask before guzzling some water.

"At least fifty more pounds."

"I hate you," I murmur, but the words don't carry any real heat.

"Come on, we both need showers. I'll make coffee while you take yours," Nixon states, but I don't want to be alone right now.

"Shower with me. It will save time."

He chuckles. "It most definitely *won't* save time. But seeing as we were up long before we have to be, we have some leeway."

I cheer like I won the bet and race toward my room.

I'm getting the shower to the right temperature when large hands grip my waist, and tickly kisses cover my shoulder. The one time I kissed a man with a beard in the past was a turn-off for me, but it's another thing that is different with Nixon.

"Your bathroom is the size of my bedroom," he whispers against my skin.

"Maybe you should get a bigger place," I tease.

"Maybe I should just stay here forever," he counters.

My spine stiffens, and I'm sure he notices because he steps away.

Forever is a word that terrifies me. This dynamic is only supposed to be temporary. Nixon was only joking, but it makes me wonder if he feels how right this is too. I'm not supposed to fall for this man. This is just sex. But fuck, it's hard to keep emotions at bay when he makes me feel whole, safe, and better than I ever have.

Without responding, I shove my shorts down and step into the hot water, letting out a contented sigh as Nixon joins me.

"I didn't mean to upset you," he says.

"You didn't." It's not a lie, but it isn't the whole truth either.

"Let me make it up to you." His tone is soft and comforting as he turns me and pulls me in for the best kiss of my life.

He licks my lips before plunging his tongue inside the second I give him access. Tingles run up my spine as his hard cock presses into my stomach, the base grazing against my erection. When he pushes even harder into me, I can't help but moan.

"I can't get enough of you," he whispers against my lips.

"The feeling's mutual," I confess, wrapping my hands around his neck and kissing him again.

How is it that I'm already so addicted to Nixon? Whatever this is, I don't want to give him up.

After we make out for a while, Nixon backs up and pulls me toward the shower bench. He sits and pulls me to straddle him, gripping our cocks in his strong hand.

"Yes," I cry out as he strokes us together. The feeling of his silky yet ridiculously hard dick against mine and the slight calluses of his fingers is almost sensory overload.

As we're making out, his hand slides up and down our cocks, and we both fuck into his fist. The kiss is needy and sloppy, desperate, but also fucking perfect. It doesn't take long before a tingle forms in my spine, and I'm almost embarrassed to admit how quickly I come, coating his chest and fist with my load.

Nixon keeps stroking us, trying to chase his release, but I pull out of his grasp to drop to my knees. "Come down my throat," I beg before covering him with my mouth.

The salty taste of his precum mixed with my release coats my tongue, making me lightheaded while I suck him deep into my mouth until I gag. This blow job is different than last night. He isn't fucking my face or forcing me deeper. Instead, he's letting me do what I feel is right, letting me take control, and honestly, I like it both ways.

I take him as deep as I can, saliva dripping around the corners of my mouth as I gag. Tears pool in my eyes, and I'm sure I look like a mess, but I don't care because every time I swallow him down, Nixon's eyes roll into the back of his head, and I love putting that look on his face.

Nixon groans out a shuddering release, filling my mouth with his salty cum. I swallow it all, not missing a drop. Lazily, I suck until Nixon is almost whimpering from it being too much, and I pull off with a pop, resting my head against his knee.

"I could use a nap after that," I tease, and a yawn slips past my lips.

"I'd love to tuck you in and hold you for a while, but you have to be at work soon," Nixon states, being the voice of reason.

"I guess we should *actually* shower, then," I murmur as he helps me up.

Nixon positions me under the spray, holding me for a minute, and drops a gentle kiss on my lips that makes my stomach flip.

I need to push back.

This is too much already, and it's only been two days. But I let myself soak up this feeling of rightness for a bit longer, telling myself I'll put the wall up again after.

I've never struggled with keeping people out of my life before.

Why is Nixon different?

Chapter 12

Nixon

My phone rings while I'm watching Dante work. He's currently holding a pretty blonde actress who is the damsel of this movie. "What's up?" I answer.

"I found something interesting," Sophy says with an almost gleeful tone.

"What would that be?"

Everything has been a dead end in this case, so there has to be something small we're missing, but I can't figure it out.

"Since we keep hitting walls everywhere we turn, I decided to interview everyone I could from the night of the red carpet."

I wonder how long that took. There were a lot of people there that night.

"Is that where you found this interesting thing you want to tell me?"

She giggles. "Obviously," she replies, her voice filled with sass.

"Are you going to divulge that information?" I ask, and she makes a raspberry into the phone.

Gross, I can literally hear her spit hitting the phone. "Make sure you wipe your phone down after that." I don't doubt she's rolling her eyes at me.

"You steal all the fun out of this," she murmurs as I watch the damsel pull Dante down for a kiss.

I'm a jealous fucker, and if I didn't know Dante wasn't into that woman at all, I'd probably be seeing green right now. It wouldn't be too good for Dante's image if his bodyguard went all *Hulk smash* over him kissing someone. Especially since Dante is so deep in the closet that he's made friends with the dust bunnies. The last thing I want is to out him when he isn't ready.

Honestly, from talking with him, I'm not sure if he'll ever be ready. Even though I won't say it out loud, I hate it.

It's been a week since we started our dynamic, and while that's fast to fall for someone, I'm already tumbling down the rabbit hole. Something I know I shouldn't do because Dante can't love me like that, but there's no stopping it. Not unless I want to end what we have, and I don't. My heart will simply be collateral damage when this all ends.

"So anyway..." Sophy's voice pulls my attention back to her. "...the interesting information I found was while talking to the interview team that was with Dante when he collapsed."

"Did they forget to tell the police something?" I'm not sure where she's going with this.

"Not really. But they told me they received an anonymous tip to ask Dante about his sexuality. They blew it off, but the guy said he wanted to tell me about it because it was weird."

I hum along in agreement that it is weird. Especially considering the guy who drugged Dante asked him about being gay.

"Thanks for the info, Soph. I'll keep it in mind while trying to piece this all together. Got anything else?"

"That's all for now. If I get more, I'll let you know," she states and ends the call.

Only a handful of people know about Dante's true sexuality, and one of them is trying to get that information out there by the sounds of it. But why? Motive here is key, and I can't figure that out yet, which pisses me off.

I'm normally good at solving puzzles like this, quickly getting to the bottom of the situation. For some reason, I still can't figure it out, even with this information.

I grab the back of my neck, watching Dante carry the damsel away before the director yells cut. The actress gives Dante a hug and skips off with a giant grin on her face while the man who is stealing my heart makes his way toward me.

I wonder if I'm having a hard time solving this case because part of me doesn't want to. The moment Dante is safe is when I have to let him go. We won't have a real reason to see each other anymore, at least not as often as we are now. I hate that thought. At the same time, I can't let my feelings for him derail my focus. He deserves the truth, and I have to be the one to find it for him, even if that means leaving him sooner than I want to.

"THANKS FOR FILLING IN for a bit," I tell Denver as he meets me on set.

A few hours are left in the day, and I want to do something special for Dante. He's going to give me shit for leaving, even for a short time, but he loves to give me a hard time. He'll get over it tonight when he's begging me to let him come. It's not like I'm leaving him in any real danger. I trust Denver with my life, so Dante is in good hands.

I trust all the people who work for me, but Denver and Bennett are my two number ones. This is why Bennett is currently at Dante's house supervising the contractors who are setting up the safe room.

Added precautions are never a bad thing, and I'm hoping it will help Dante feel safe in his own house.

"No problem, man. You should probably take a full day off soon. You don't normally work this much," he notes.

"I'm fine. No one in Dante's circle knows I'm with him full time. We have to keep it that way until we know what the fuck is going on. If I randomly drop in at his house, it makes sense. If you do, it doesn't."

Denver grabs the back of his neck but nods. "I guess I see your point. Are you any closer to solving the case?"

"Not really. Soph found something small, but it doesn't help much if I'm being honest."

"Well, if you need any help, I'm here. Are you sure you're okay? You're taking on a lot more of this case than you normally do. Why don't you delegate more?"

"I've got this," I inform him, changing the subject because he knows me too well. "I'll be back before Dante finishes." I turn on my heels after he nods at me.

Getting away from Denver quickly was the smart move because the second he started to pry would be when it all blew up. He'd see what's lying under the surface, and I can't let that happen. I promised to keep Dante's secret to myself. I'll be damned if he has to deal with that before he's ready.

"How'd it go?" I ask Denver but keep my eyes on Dante, who is wiping the sweat off his brow with a towel an assistant handed him.

"Good, nothing to report," Denver replies with a smile. "If you ever need me to fill in, just let me know. Although it will be nice when you don't have to be full time with Dante anymore so you can come out for beers again," he teases as Dante walks over to us.

"I miss you guys too, but it's important that I keep the client safe." I regret the word choice immediately when Dante's face falls.

"I get it. Honestly, I'd like another full-time client. They're a great challenge. Thankfully, with most of them, though, we still get breaks."

"I know. The next one we get will be all yours. Although I'll hate that I can't have you on call for me anymore."

He laughs and waves as he heads off.

"Why didn't you tell me Denver was taking your place for a bit?" Dante grumbles, pulling a bottle of water out of our cooler.

"Didn't want to argue with you," I state because it's the truth.

He narrows his eyes at me but doesn't say anything.

"Are you getting sick of your *client* already?" he bites out.

I clench my jaw, wishing I could prove to him right now that he means more to me than that, but we're in public.

"I'm not sick of you. I just wanted to pick up a few things for tonight."

His eyes go wide, and he loses his angry expression, but it quickly returns.

"Whatever." He scoffs, pushing past me to head to his trailer.

"You know you're more than just a client to me," I tell him when we are in the privacy of his trailer. "But I didn't want to out you and tell Denver we're fucking. What did you want me to say?" I make sure to keep my voice low in case someone is close by listening.

Dante shakes his head and blows out a breath.

"Sorry. You're right. I'm just tired."

"What do you want for dinner? You're going to need a big meal for the plans I have for tonight."

Dante bites his lip and gets naked, making sure to go slow enough to tease me. "Why don't you pick? That way, you can make sure I have something to your liking." He wiggles his ass at me.

His gaze drops to my hand rearranging my hardening cock, and his tongue slips out, sweeping his bottom lip. *Fuck, I am going to have fun edging him tonight.* If he keeps this up, his ass will be cherry red. My hand is already itching.

As soon as he's ready, we make our way to the car, and it takes everything I have to keep the mask of professionalism in place. I would love nothing more than to push him up against the passenger door and remind him how much more he is than a client. Instead, I take a deep breath and slide into the driver's seat.

It's not until a mile or so down the road that one of us finally speaks, the sexual tension thick in the confined space.

"Do you know of anyone who would want to out you? Someone who would gain something from that?" I ask Dante, careful to keep my eyes on the road.

"No." He gasps, turning in his seat to stare at me with wide eyes. "Why would anyone want to do that?"

I can't get what Sophy said out of my head.

"The team that interviewed you after you got drugged was sent a tip to ask you about your sexuality." He frowns and looks out the window.

Shit, I didn't mean to upset him again.

"Jeramiah might want to out me," he whispers, mentioning his ex. "He hates my dad, and considering Dad is running for office, there is a possibility that he wants to out me to fuck with the results..." He pauses and looks at me with sad eyes. "But I can't see him wanting me dead."

Dante's words cause a light bulb to go off in my head, and I want to kick myself for not thinking about this earlier.

"What if whoever's behind this didn't want you dead?" I question as I take a left turn.

"Where are we going?" Dante asks.

"My office. I want to pull up your tox reports."

"I'm so confused right now. If they didn't want me dead, why drug me?" he asks, but I don't respond in case I'm wrong.

If I *am* right, this changes *everything*.

Chapter 13

Dante

NIXON'S PLACE OF BUSINESS is dark, giving off an eerie feel when we enter. "I'm surprised you don't have people working late," I state as we make our way to his office.

"We are all workaholics here, but most work from home after hours. I'd be doing the same, but I don't have your tox report saved to my laptop, and I didn't back it up to the cloud."

"What exactly are you hoping to gain from reading the report again?" I inquire as he sits down, boots up his computer, and pats his lap.

I love that he wants to keep me close, so I rush over and sit down, leaning my head against his shoulder.

"I want to see what the numbers are. Then I'm going to call a friend, who's a doctor, and ask if there's a possibility that whoever did this didn't mean to almost kill you."

My eyebrows shoot up to my hairline, and I sit up straight. "What did they want to do if they didn't want to kill me?"

"Get you messy, make you lose your inhibitions, and answer questions about your sexuality."

"Holy shit," I murmur, almost not believing his words. "So maybe it *was* Jeramiah?" I question, snuggling back into Nixon, wanting his body to give me comfort.

"I still don't know. Obviously, he has motive, but I'm not ruling anyone out yet," Nixon states as he types away.

It doesn't take him long to pull up the report and look over the numbers. All of it is gibberish to me, but Nixon seems like he understands it.

After he's absorbed the information, he pulls his phone out and calls his friend, putting it on speaker, which makes me smile. He isn't doing anything behind my back. He's including me in all of this, and for some reason, that makes me feel extra special. Like we're a team or something.

Shit. Why does he have to treat me so well? Couldn't he just be a grumpy asshole when we aren't fucking?

Feelings are dangerous.

I don't want them.

"Hey, Nixon, what's up?" a male greets on the other end of the line.

"Hey, Dax. Just wondering if you have a moment to give me your medical expertise," Nixon replies.

"Sure, just give me a second. I'll head to my office. Izzy has Caidance over, and they are gabbing up a storm." He chuckles.

I have no idea who these people are, but Nixon nods in understanding.

"Okay, I'm alone. What can I help you with?"

"I'm working on a case where a client of mine was drugged. He almost died, so we thought it was an attempted murder, but I'm wondering if there is another possibility."

"What does his toxicology report look like?"

Nixon responds with big words and numbers that mean nothing to me.

"I was curious if maybe someone wanted to intoxicate my client enough to get him to admit to something but accidentally went overboard."

The doctor hums on the other end of the phone but doesn't respond right away. "That's definitely a possibility. Drugs are a finicky thing and easy to mess up, especially without knowing the real dose. When you buy shit off the streets, there is no way of knowing what's actually in it. I doubt whoever did this got their supplies anywhere reputable."

Nixon nods even though the guy can't see him.

"Thanks, Dax. That confirms my suspicions. Now I can work this case from a different angle."

"No problem," Dax responds, his voice sounding like he's smiling. "Happy I could be of some help. I hope you can solve this quickly for your client."

What happens when Nixon does solve the case?

Does that mean what we have will end?

I mean, that's what we discussed at the beginning. I won't have a reason to see him as often as I do now, but the idea of only being with him once in a blue moon doesn't sit right with me. I don't want this to end.

I want more.

"Me too," Nixon tells Dax, his words pulling me from my spiraling thoughts, and my heart aches.

Maybe Nixon does want this to end. Maybe he's had his fill of me.

What would a guy like Nixon want permanently with a guy like me, anyway? He's out and proud, and I'm as deep in the closet as it gets. I can't offer him anything healthy long-term, yet I want to.

What would be the worst thing that could happen if I came out?

A fuck load of shit, actually, but would it be worth it?

MY BRAIN WON'T STOP playing a million things over in my head. It's fucking exhausting, a combination of what-ifs and wondering who the hell wants to out me. The only person I can think of is Jeramiah, but Nixon doesn't seem convinced.

"If someone just wants to out me and not kill me, why did they break into the house?" I ask when we get inside my home, kicking off my shoes and letting a few of my thoughts out.

"You weren't supposed to be here that night. Maybe they were only trying to get information. Find something worth sharing with the media."

"I don't understand why my sexuality is anyone's fucking business," I yell, everything becoming too much and bubbling over.

Nixon rushes to me and wraps his arms around my shoulders. "It's not, but people suck. They only care about themselves," he whispers into my hair. "If they can do something to push themselves farther along or get revenge, they'll do it, not caring who is collateral damage."

I nod against his chest as a few tears trail down my cheek. I'm normally not a crier, but I'm so over all of this. It's too much. But thankfully, Nixon is here. Somehow, he helps me forget, but the heavy thoughts creep in.

How long is that going to be for?

A frightful thought pushes its way to the forefront of my mind, and I pull away to look into Nixon's eyes. "Are you going to move out now that I'm not in danger?" I pray the answer is no. I'm not ready to let him go yet. It's already going to be over sooner than I'd like.

"Do you want me to?" he asks, moving his right hand from my back to my chin, trailing his thumb along my lip.

"I'm not sure…" I lie, letting my words trail off. I know what I want, but I can't seem to voice the words.

I'm not supposed to be falling for him.

"How about we make that decision another day," he suggests before leaning down to kiss me gently.

It's like a weight has been lifted off my shoulders, and I melt into him. He's not leaving, at least not yet.

"Can I get your mind off of everything?" Nixon asks after a few incredible kisses.

"What do you have in mind?" I inquire, completely intrigued by the idea.

"I had this idea randomly pop into my head about tying you down and flogging your perfect body. I also want to edge you a little, so remember, no coming until I say."

My breath hitches, and I gasp. "Why does that sound so hot?"

He smirks and kneads my hips where he's still holding me. "It's okay to have kinks that not everyone has. It's fine to be physically turned on by pain. It's more than okay to crave it as well. It doesn't make you weird to think this is extremely hot," he assures me, reaching for my hand and placing it on his crotch. "As you can tell, I'm just as turned on as you are."

"Take me to bed, Sir," I whisper before reaching up on my tiptoes to kiss him again. "And make it hurt." I chuckle when I hear Nixon groan behind me after I turn to strut to our room, making sure to sway my hips more than usual.

I bet his eyes are glued to my ass. That's the goal, anyway.

A swat on my ass has me yelping but also laughing. "Stop being a tease, Brat."

I pause, peering at him over my shoulder. "Make me," I goad in a husky voice. The way Nixon's eyes turn almost deadly has my cock throbbing between my legs.

This is going to be amazing. At least for a short time, I'll be able to think of nothing but this man.

Chapter 14

Nixon

BEFORE COMMANDING DANTE TO strip, I grab the bag of items I purchased today. He obeys without smart-mouthing me, making it obvious he needs a mental release, and I'm happy to give it to him. While he gets naked, I install the under-the-mattress restraints.

"On the bed," I state firmly when I'm done.

Dante climbs on eagerly, and I secure his wrists and ankles with soft cuffs, ensuring they aren't too tight and his circulation isn't being cut off, and also that they don't allow him to break free.

"How does that feel?" I ask him, double-checking that the cuffs aren't cutting into his skin and he's comfortable.

"Good." He gives me a slight grin, his eyes heated with desire.

I return his smile as I step back and take a moment to soak him in. His cock is as hard as a rock resting against his stomach, and the sight makes my mouth water. His creamy skin is so perfect right now, but I can't wait to tarnish it a little. I'll make sure not to get too carried away, not wanting him to have to explain marks to his director. Thankfully, he has two days off, giving him time to recover and allowing the marks to fade before he returns to work.

Reaching into the bag, I pull out a flogger, giving my hand a few good slaps, testing the sting. Dante's eyes go wide, and his chest rises and falls a little quicker as his breathing picks up. I bet his heart is racing. I know mine is just from the anticipation.

"What are your safe words?" I ask before we start the scene. I want to make sure we are still using the traffic light system but also get an idea of where his head is.

"Green is go, yellow is slow down, and red is stop," he informs me, his words almost too rushed to understand him through his panting.

"Good boy. What are you feeling right now?"

"Green, Sir," he replies with a grin.

"Perfect, now let's get started," I murmur, strutting closer to him.

To start, I set the flogger on his left shoulder, gently dragging it across his chest to his right hip before doing the same to the other side, taking my time tickling his body, letting the leather tails trail across his skin.

His body shivers, and his cock bobs against his stomach, leaving a tiny trail of precum.

As I drag the flogger across his body a few more times, I make sure to avoid his cock for the time being.

"I need more," Dante says.

"Patience, Treasure."

He takes a deep breath as the flogger slips down his leg, tickling his inner thigh on the upstroke. His legs shake a little, and his body trying to fight against the restraints makes me smirk. I love having this effect on him.

After I'm done teasing him, I lift my arm and bring it down hard against his left thigh, causing him to cry out and bow his back. I do the same to his right thigh, taking in the way his skin turns a glorious shade of bright red.

"Fuck," Dante yells when I bring the flogger down on his cock.

I pause for a moment, studying him. "Too much?" I ask, checking in with him while gently dragging the flogger across his chest.

Dante shakes his head. "More," he begs, and my cock pushes against my pants so hard I'm afraid the zipper might break.

I flog him repeatedly, making sure I don't hit the same spot twice until he's a whimpering mess, begging me to let him come.

"You did so fucking good," I praise as I ditch the flogger.

Before climbing onto the bed, I take a step back to appreciate the rosy glow of his once-pale skin. It's no longer pristine and unmarked, and the fact I did that makes my cock ache.

Lying next to him, I leave him restrained and kiss him with all of the passion I have while stroking his cock.

I want to tell him how I feel and that I'm falling for him.

How I don't ever want to leave him...

... but I can't.

It would destroy what we have. Dante made it clear what this was. Feelings were never supposed to be involved. While he doesn't want me to leave, I can't fool myself into thinking it means more.

"Come for me, Treasure," I whisper against his neck, picking up the speed of my hand.

With a roar, Dante explodes, coating my hand, his chest and stomach, even getting a little on his chin. Then I move to release his limbs before heading to the bathroom to get a warm cloth. As soon as he's cleaned up, I grab his aftercare supplies and something new I picked up today.

"Is that a stuffy?" Dante asks after I strip my clothes and climb into bed with him.

"It is. I know you said you wanted one, so I thought I'd surprise you," I say, then bring the straw I placed in a glass of juice to his lips.

He squeezes the duck plushie while sipping. There is a drunk expression on his face, but an extremely satisfied one.

"You didn't get to come," Dante mentions before I place a chunk of KitKat in his mouth.

"Tonight wasn't about me. It was about you."

He nods but doesn't say anything.

"How are you feeling? Did I do anything you didn't like?"

Dante shakes his head, his hair tickling my chin. It makes me wonder if he would grow it out after this movie. The idea of being able to wrap my hand around it and pull while I fuck him has me stifling a groan. It's definitely something we should talk about. "I'm feeling really good. I loved it all. Honestly, I wouldn't mind even more one day. Maybe after this movie is over."

"You want to continue this that far?" I ask, my heart rate picking up.

Can he hear how loud it's beating?

"I like what we have," he states. "I'm not sure about the logistics of it all once you move out, but we could probably figure something out, right?"

I nod, but a million questions are on the tip of my tongue.

Am I willing to take any scraps he'll give me?

Is what we have enough for me in the long run?

I agreed to what this is, but that was before I fell. Now I want him to be my boyfriend. I want to take him out on dates and take him home to meet my parents one day. All of which isn't possible.

Fuck, I hate this.

DANTE'S PHONE WAKES US the next morning, but it's obvious it isn't early by the amount of sunlight beaming through the window.

"Hello?" Dante answers groggily.

"You're still sleeping?" Elanor asks with a gasp.

His phone isn't on speaker, but I can hear every word with us being so close.

"Stayed up late last night. I have two days off, so I didn't think it was a big deal."

"Of course. I want to come over today to go over some upcoming events and a few other things. Does this afternoon work for you?"

"Should I invite Nixon? I'm sure he'll want to know about the events." I smile.

"I'll talk to him about it after. Besides, I thought you didn't get along with him, or is that changing?"

"He's still a pain in my ass, but I'm positive he'll bitch if he misses this meeting. Please don't make me go through that." He groans, and I bite my knuckle to stop the laugh that wants to break out.

"Fine. Invite the bodyguard," she murmurs, and Dante's smile widens.

"Okay, cool, I'll send him a text right now. Talk soon," he tells her and ends the call.

"You're a good actor," I say, rolling onto him.

My thighs rest on the outside of his, and I hold my weight on my forearms before kissing him. Our hard cocks rub together, no barriers separating us, and the feel of his velvety skin pulls a moan from me.

"Gah." Dante groans as I grind against him.

"How are you feeling after last night?" I ask.

Dante narrows his eyes at me. "Is now really the time to ask?"

"No time like the present," I reply nonchalantly.

"I'm fine, but I would really like more than just your dick rubbing against me."

I lift a brow, waiting for a secret word.

"Please, Sir... can I have some more?"

I chuckle and slide off him, moving us so we are facing each other before gripping us both in my hand.

"Yes," Dante pants while I stroke us together, his hips bucking into my grip.

I slip my tongue into his mouth as we make out, and it doesn't take long for us to explode.

"We need a shower," I mention after we cuddle for a few moments, both of us sticky from our cum.

"I don't wanna move," Dante complains.

I kiss the top of his head. "I know, Treasure, but Elanor is coming over this afternoon. I still need to feed you and move the SUV out of the garage before she shows up."

"Fine..." He groans. "But can I have a shower blow job?"

I laugh. "How are you ready to go again?"

"I'm young. I recover quickly," he quips.

"Come on, get up. I guess a shower blow job could be arranged," I concede.

"You're the best. I think I'm going to keep you forever," Dante jokes before leaping out of bed and racing to the bathroom.

I take my time following because the word 'forever' makes me wish that was possible. I guess, in some ways, it is if I'm okay with no one ever knowing about us. But I don't think I am. This relationship has to have an end date, but no matter if that date is tomorrow, a week, a month, or even years from now, I'll be left broken. And I'm the only one to blame.

Chapter 15

Dante

No matter where I am or what I'm doing, I always find myself searching for Nixon. It's something I noticed shortly after we started whatever the hell *this* is.

While I'm acting, I keep my focus on task, but the second the director calls 'cut,' my eyes make a beeline for Nixon. It made me nervous at first. What if someone caught on? I mean, it would be easy enough to come up with a lie. I've been doing that my entire career. Hell, half the time I'm not sure if I am even capable of telling the truth anymore.

Nixon and I have been waiting for Elanor in the living room—him in the recliner working on his laptop and me on the couch, *trying* to watch a show but constantly getting distracted and staring at the sexy man.

"Anything interesting going on at work?" I question, done pretending I can pay attention to the show.

Nixon shakes his head and rubs the back of his neck. "Not really. Just been trying to get some of the boring shit done for the week. Being the boss sucks sometimes."

"Yeah. I wouldn't want to be in charge of other people. That sounds way too stressful."

"I don't mind being in charge. It's just all the bullshit that comes with owning a business that gets taxing at times."

"Makes sense. Can't you just get other people to do that shit?"

"Some of it. But I'm also a control freak, so it's hard to delegate."

"You... a control freak? I never would have guessed," I say in mock surprise.

"Brat," Nixon jokes, picking up the Kleenex box next to him and gently tossing it at me.

I'm about to make a remark about how he loves it when the doorbell rings, cutting off our friendly banter. I don't even bother getting off the couch, knowing Nixon will chew me out if I open the door.

"Since when do you lock the door?" Elanor asks after Nixon lets her in.

"Since someone tried to kill me," I reply with an expression that should read *duh*.

Elanor giggles. "I guess that makes sense."

The way she ignores Nixon kind of irks me, but I don't want to say anything that could bring on questions I don't have answers to.

"What all do we have to go over?" I ask as Elanor sits down next to me.

"Let's start with the scheduled appearances first, then move on to everything else," she states.

I nod, not caring what order we do this in, just wanting to get it over with. My heart isn't in it today. I'd rather be simply Dante, not Dante, the actor. Actually, I'd like to spend more time alone with Nixon, but I can't tell her that.

Nixon sits back in his chair, listening intently while Elanor goes on and on about the events I *have* to attend in the next couple of months. My skin crawls at the idea alone. I'll no longer have Anna to be with me to help ease my anxiety, and I'm not sure how I am going to get through anything without her. Maybe I'll call a doctor to get a prescription for something.

As soon as everything is all in place, we move on to what's next for my career and image.

"So I've been talking with Anna. We think six months after the breakup would be a good time for her to do an interview coming out of the closet." I nod, unsure of what that has to do with my career and image. "I was thinking it might be a good time for you to come out as well," she says with a bright smile like she doesn't know me at all. "We could even set up a double interview so you can both come out at the same time."

I shake my head. "I'm not ready, Elanor. You should know that. I'm not sure I'll ever be ready." Tears prickle my eyes.

Elanor's face contorts for a moment, almost like she's taken aback that I told her no. Obviously, that isn't something I do often. "Of course, honey," Elanor says, trying to console me. "I'm sorry. I shouldn't have brought it up. I just thought maybe you'd see Anna taking this step and want to do the same."

"I don't," I snap.

Elanor backs off, eyes wide in shock, but her soft smile returns quickly. "Well, whenever you're ready, let me know."

I cast my eyes to the floor. She's never pushed for this before.

That's when it hits me.

Holy shit...

I think Elanor is the 'insider.'

What the fuck? Why does she want me to come out of the closet? What does she have to gain from that? Wouldn't she want her friend to be ready before pushing them to do something like this?

I've never wanted to come out publicly and never thought I would, but things are changing. I wish I could live a life where I have a man who loves me and stay in the closet at the same time. But that isn't fair to anyone. I must let Nixon go one day or overcome my fear and come out. Both scare the shit out of me.

"Anything else we need to talk about?" I ask in a clipped tone, letting Elanor know I'm done with this meeting.

"Not today," she says, standing. "Take care, sweetheart. We'll talk soon."

As soon as Nixon locks the door behind Elanor, he makes his way over to me and wraps his arms around me.

"Do you think Elanor is the one who is trying to out me?" I whisper into his shirt.

He nods while rubbing my back. "I just don't know what she has to gain from you coming out."

I wish I had the answer to that as well.

"Now what do I do?" I pull away so I can stare into his eyes.

"Right now, you don't have to do anything. Why don't we focus on anything but all this bullshit? Tomorrow, we'll come up with a plan."

I like the idea of pretending that doom isn't lurking around the corner. Unfortunately, I'm better at putting blinders on than facing anything head-on.

Tonight, we'll pretend that everything is perfect.

"What should we do tonight?" I ask, wanting Nixon to take control.

"How about we watch a movie?"

"That seems rather boring."

He chuckles. "I've got a way to keep it entertaining."

That piques my interest. "Do tell."

Nixon places his hand under my chin and leans down for a gentle kiss, but it turns heated when his tongue licks the seam of my lips.

"We're going to watch the movie while you sit on my cock," he advises. My dick thickens in my pants, and my heart races.

"I think I could get behind that," I say with a smirk.

"I didn't even get to the good part." I'm dying to know what he's thinking. "You're not allowed to move. You're just there to keep me warm and deal with every time I decide to readjust or fuck up into you. If you're a good little cock warmer, once the movie is over, I'll fuck you so hard you'll see stars. If you disobey or come before I say so, you'll be punished."

I gulp, trying to come up with a response, but my brain is empty. I hate the fact that I won't be able to move, but I love that he wants to use me like this. It's oddly a huge turn-on.

"What do you think?" Nixon asks. "Want to Netflix and chill?"

I take a deep breath, staring him in the eyes. "Yes, Sir."

Nixon heads to the bedroom, returning with some supplies, and takes my hand, guiding me to the theater room. Then he turns to stare intently into my eyes. "Strip," he commands, placing the bottle of lube and a few packets of condoms beside a chair.

I do exactly as I'm told, watching as he does the same, my eyes wandering over his incredible body.

How did I get so lucky to get the hottest bodyguard ever?

As soon as we are both naked, Nixon sits in one of the large recliners and taps the ottoman in front of him.

"Lean over this and queue up a movie," he instructs.

I move toward him, wondering what he has in mind but wanting to obey. That's something I've noticed about myself recently. I find myself wanting to obey Nixon more. I still enjoy pushing his buttons but no longer want to fight him at every step. I'm not sure what that means, though.

While I'm looking through Netflix, Nixon pushes a lubed-up finger against my hole, and I pause.

"Keep looking, Treasure," he tells me as he gently shoves the digit inside.

I moan but continue searching. Maybe if I find a movie quickly, I could sit back and enjoy Nixon stretching me.

"This looks good," I murmur, clicking on a random movie.

"I'm not really in the mood for a comedy," he says, pressing a second finger in. "Pick something else."

I take a deep breath as he scissors his fingers. *How am I supposed to pick a movie when I can't see straight?* Not wanting to argue because I don't want him to stop, I look for something else, taking my time because I have a strong suspicion he won't be in the 'mood' for whatever I choose until I'm good and stretched.

The ottoman is getting sticky beneath me as my precum leaks, but I'm trying my hardest to focus on finding a good movie. That is until Nixon moves his fingers to hit my prostate.

"Fuck," I cry out, my eyes slamming shut from euphoria.

Nixon takes that moment to shove in a third finger, and fuck, it's phenomenal to feel so full.

"Have you picked a movie?" he asks, his voice forcing me to open my eyes.

"Is an action movie okay?" I question, hovering over one I've been wanting to watch for a while.

"That looks perfect, Treasure," he says before gently pulling his fingers from me, leaving me empty and wanting. "Now, come sit on my lap like a good cock warmer."

I get up and turn to see Nixon stroking his giant sheathed cock with lube. *Fuck, I want that in me right now.* Turning back around, I lower myself onto the world's hottest bodyguard's lap.

With a firm grip on my hip, Nixon guides me onto his erection, and I blow out a breath while relaxing so I can take him in. Thanks to the stretching, it doesn't take long until I'm completely seated, and I lean back against his chest.

"Turn the movie on," Nixon whispers into my ear, giving a small buck of his hips and eliciting a moan from me.

"The remote is too far away," I reply breathlessly.

"I can fix that." He edges us to the end of the recliner and leans forward to grab the remote.

The angle has his cock pressing into me in the most glorious way, and I swear my eyes roll into the back of my head.

This movie is going to be delicious torture.

I know it.

Chapter 16

Nixon

IT'S OBVIOUS DANTE IS fighting the urge to move so hard, especially when I whisper kisses against his neck or when I flex my hips, teasing him by pushing my cock further into him. It's like his body is humming with desire.

"How are you liking the movie?" I whisper in his ear before nibbling on the lobe.

"It's good," he murmurs after inhaling a deep breath.

"Who's your favorite character?" I'm pretty sure he isn't paying close attention.

"Um... the main guy..." he responds, panting, and I chuckle. "Fuuuck... when you laugh, I can *feel* your cock move."

"What about when I do this?" I buck my hips, gripping him hard, ensuring I'm as deep as I can go.

"Gah!"

I reach around him, grasping his cock and swiping my thumb against the tip before letting go. Then, lifting my thumb to his lips, I encourage him to suck the precum off, moaning at the feel of his mouth around my thumb. "Fuck, Treasure. Taste how good you are. I love how you drip. And you taste so fucking good."

Pulling my thumb from his mouth, I release a low groan, then grip his chin. I turn his face and kiss him hard, shoving my tongue into his mouth and tasting him. The growl that rumbles through my chest is deep, filled with unadulterated lust. This man is an addiction, and I'm dying for a fix, but this is for him.

"I need you," he whimpers against my lips.

I blow out a breath, trying to regain control. "Soon, Treasure. The second that movie's over, I'll bend you over the ottoman and fuck you as hard as I can."

He nods and takes a deep breath, resting his head against my chest again. Then the second the credits start to roll, I push Dante forward. He braces himself on the ottoman, and I buck into him with all I have.

"Yes," he cries out as I grasp his throat gently, not squeezing yet.

"Do you still want to try this?" I ask, needing his verbal confirmation before we go ahead with this.

"Yes, Sir," he responds eagerly. I press into the sides of his neck firmer, squeezing with just the right amount of pressure.

"You were such a good boy," I praise, reaching around and stroking his cock in time with each thrust. "Are you ready to come?" I ask as a tingle forms in the base of my spine.

"Yes... Sir," he pants out, whimpering as I pick up my speed, chasing my orgasm.

I've been on edge as much as Dante has this entire movie, and I'm not going to last long. His ass gripping my cock while we cuddled was heaven and hell all wrapped together.

Panting, moaning, and skin slapping fills the theater room, the music of the movie's end credits fading into the background.

"Come for me, Treasure," I command moments before exploding into the condom, wishing it was his ass so I could watch my cum drip out of him.

"Shit," Dante yells as he reaches his climax, covering the ottoman in thick ropes of cum.

We collapse, trying to catch our breath, not moving for who knows how long.

"Let's go take a shower," I suggest when I've gained the ability to speak again. "I'll clean the ottoman later."

"Fuck no. I'll just buy a new one," Dante mutters as I pull out of him.

"Deal." I chuckle, walking with him to our room.

"How did you get so good at sex?" he asks as he leans against the door frame, waiting for me to warm the shower up and dispose of my condom. "Years of practice," I answer, seeing no reason to lie.

"I feel like I should be jealous, but I kind of want to thank your exes. Why aren't you in a committed relationship? You're a catch."

"I'm kind of married to my job. Most guys don't like the fact that I could be called away at any moment. I've never slept with a client before." My confession makes Dante's eyes go wide. "You make me break all kinds of rules." That brings a smile to his gorgeous face. "You're special," I add. His face falls, but I don't understand why. "What's wrong?" I rush to him.

"I'm not good enough for you," he whispers.

"That's not true at all."

"It is true, Nixon. You're an amazing man who has his life together and is proud of who he is. I'm a twenty-four-year-old poser terrified to come out."

"We all go through our journey at our own pace. It's different for everyone. With your upbringing, it makes sense why you've stayed in the closet for so long. No one should force you to come out until you're ready."

"But Elanor is trying to do just that," he counters, eyes shining with unshed tears, breaking my heart.

"We'll figure out a way to stop her." Truth be told, I have no idea how we're going to accomplish that. She's been trying to get Dante to fess up or out himself by accident, but with that not working, I don't see anything stopping her from leaking the knowledge she has.

Dante closes his eyes, breathing in deeply before slowly letting it out.

"Come on, let's get cleaned up. I'm tired," he states, changing the subject.

The shower doesn't take long, and before I know it, we are in bed, but even though Dante is wrapped in my arms, he feels distant. He's pulling away already.

I need to figure out a way to make this work.

As much as I didn't want to let myself fall, it happened. I'm in love with Dante Michaelson, and I don't want to let him go. I'll figure out a way to live in the closet with him if I have to, but first, I have to make sure he doesn't push me away.

THE BUZZING OF DANTE'S phone wakes us up, and I turn to watch him answer it. This is becoming a habit I don't care for.

"Hey, beautiful, how is Paris?" Dante answers, and I know it's Anna.

He nods along while she talks, but the smile he's trying to put on so she doesn't clue into other things going on doesn't reach his eyes.

"I'm fine," he tells her, but it doesn't sound like a genuine response, and she must not buy it because he huffs out a breath.

"You can tell her," I share quietly, and his eyes go wide.

"Actually, I'm not okay." He takes a deep breath and relays the entire story of what has been happening in his life since the drugging, leaving out the detail that we have been together.

He's quiet while Anna says something, and he shakes his head before looking at me.

"Can I put you on speaker phone?" he asks and clicks a button after she responds. "What is the plan going forward?" Dante asks me.

"That's what I just asked you. I don't know what to do here," Anna grumbles. "What if we both fire Elanor? Threaten that if she goes public with the details, we'll deny it and ruin her. If she ever wants to work in the business again, she'll keep her mouth shut."

The idea actually isn't bad.

"That could work," I respond, and Anna gasps.

"What the hell is Nixon doing there in the middle of the night?"

"We're kind of fooling around," Dante tells her, appearing tense.

The words make what we have sound cheap. It's more than fooling around for me, but maybe it's not for Dante. I thought he was starting to feel things for me too, but perhaps I was blinded by my own love.

"Okay... I don't have time to process all of this, so you can fill me in more later. For now, let's work out a plan for Elanor."

"There isn't anything foolproof stopping Elanor from outing you, but if she loves her job, she should keep quiet. There is a strong possibility she was doing this to further her career in some way," I state, and Dante nods.

"When do you want to do this?" Dante asks Anna.

"Now. I'm not letting that bitch represent me for a second longer. There are a million agencies we can go with."

"Fuck. I don't want to make this call," he complains.

"How about I call her for both of us? I'll send you a text when I'm done. You can send her an email canceling her services after."

"Deal," Dante agrees.

They say quick goodbyes and then hang up. The second Dante's phone is on the nightstand, he crawls under the covers and into my arms.

"I'm sorry you're going through this," I whisper as I rub his back.

"I thought Elanor was our friend. The idea that after all this time, she'd betray our trust is too much. And not just mine, but Anna's too. Why? To push her career in another direction? Or for more money? It's just..." He pauses, struggling to speak, and lets out a sigh. "It's just a lot."

I kiss his forehead, not knowing what to say next. I want to ask Dante to be my boyfriend and tell him how I truly feel, but I'm still not sure where he is at. Hell, I don't even know how much longer he is going to want me with him.

I'm going to have to file a report and end the full-time services soon, so it wouldn't make sense for me to be here all the time. If someone was paying close attention, that could raise flags.

I hold him for a while before his phone pings, then he takes a deep breath and reads the message.

"She's fired," he whispers.

I hold him tightly, again at a loss for words. Life is going to return to normal for Dante real soon, and I haven't figured out how we will make this work going forward.

"We have a few things we need to talk about," I tell Dante as we sit down to eat breakfast.

"Do we have to?" he whines.

I give him a soft smile as I nod. "Now that we know the truth about everything happening, I have to file a report for the company. It doesn't make sense for you to have a live-in bodyguard anymore. I'll leave out *why* Elanor was doing everything. Say something along the lines of she was trying to leak a secret of yours but wanted you to do it. We also need to do a bit more research to fully connect her to the drugging, but Sophy is great at hacking. Hopefully, with the information we have, she will be able to tie the two together."

"That makes sense. What about our dynamic?" Dante questions, and I take a deep breath.

"You have to be the one to make that decision," I tell him.

"I don't want anything to change. You can cut the full-time bodyguard contract with your company, but we've been hiding it from everyone I'm close to this entire time. Why can't we hide it from your friends too? Anna's been on me for a long time to get a bodyguard. Wouldn't it make sense for you to still come to work with me? You can stay here, and we can continue what we have."

I think it over, wanting to say yes, but is it fair to both of us?

"Don't leave me, Nixon," Dante begs, reaching for my hand after I'm silent for a moment too long.

It breaks my resolve, and I say, "I'm falling for you."

When I look into his eyes, they are so fucking wide it's almost comical.

"It was never supposed to be more than just physical," he whispers.

"I tried to keep my feelings in check. I just wanted to be honest with you."

"You aren't the only one who couldn't keep his heart in a cage," he confesses with glassy eyes.

It's my turn for my eyes to go wide. "So now what?"

"I don't know, Nixon. I can't offer you more than this. I'm still not ready to come out. It's not fair to you. You deserve someone better than me."

"I don't think that's true. I'm willing to try this and see what we can build."

"What if I never come out?"

"Honestly, I'm still not sure of that answer, but I know what you can give me."

"I want to give you more," he whispers.

I don't respond, not knowing how. The words sound great, but I don't think he truly means them. In the end, Dante is comfortable being in the closet, and I have to be okay with that.

Chapter 17
Dante

NIXON'S PHONE BUZZES FOR what feels like the hundredth time, and I can't help but glare at it. "Who keeps blowing up your phone?"

We're cuddling in the theater room after a mind-blowing impact session that involved a literal paddle on my ass. I'm sure I'll be feeling it for at *least* a few days, which I love.

"Denver and the guys. They want me to come out for a beer. They've been bitching for a couple days now."

That almost makes me want to laugh. "Then why don't you go? I don't need a babysitter anymore. It would probably be healthy for our relationship if things started going back to normal. Don't get me wrong, I love having you with me all the time, but space and friendships are good too."

"I think I'm just used to you needing me. I'm also scared something is going to happen if I leave," Nixon admits, and it warms me that he's worried about me.

"It's been almost a month since we fired Elanor. If she was going to do something, wouldn't she have done it by now?"

He sighs. "Stop being right," he grumbles, and I laugh.

"Go have a few beers with the boys, and maybe I'll video chat with Anna."

"Okay," he concedes and kisses me. "I'll be two hours max."

"Take your time. I'm not going anywhere."

He gives me another kiss before walking out of the theater room.

It's been surprising to me how easy everything with Nixon has been. We've fallen into this comfortable routine, and life is almost perfect.

I never in a million years thought I would let anyone close enough to have a relationship with. But Nixon broke down all my walls, and I don't think I could picture my life without him. He wants me for me. Besides a small group of people, I don't think I've ever experienced that before.

I'm in love with Nixon.

I'm going to tell him soon.

ANNA AND I FOUND a fantastic company to represent us that handles literally everything we could ever need. I was offered a personal assistant but declined the offer for now. However, Anna jumped at the bit, saying she didn't want to use that title as a shield for her relationship with Brittany. I'm so happy for her and can't wait for her to come home in a couple of weeks.

"I miss your stupid face," Anna grumbles when she answers the FaceTime call.

"But it's right here," I tease, framing my face with my hands.

"Smartass."

"That's why you love me." I blow a kiss at her, and she rolls her eyes.

"Nixon would spank me for that."

She giggles. "How is that going?"

A goofy grin pulls at my lips. "So good. I'm really happy."

"I'm happy for you. I never thought I'd see the day that you let someone in," she states.

"Me either. Fate really took the reins here."

"Well, you deserve to be happy…" She pauses. "You are happy, right?"

"Why wouldn't I be? Everything is perfect." I'm a little confused by her questioning.

"I started feeling restless about being in the closet after Brittany and I were together for a while. I know we are different people, but I was just checking, is all."

"Nixon says he's fine with me being in the closet," I say, a little too defensively.

"Then that's great." She gives me a genuine smile. "I really am over the moon for you as long as you're truly happy. You know that's all I care about."

She is such a good friend.

"It's great to have someone like you in my corner," I remind her.

"Forever and always. I might be in love with Brittany, but you're my person. You're stuck with me forever."

I chuckle because I feel the same.

"Did you ever figure out why Brittany was acting off?" I ask, realizing with everything that has happened, I forgot to bring it up.

"I think so…" she trails off but has the goofiest grin on her face.

"Okay, are you going to tell me?"

She shakes her head. "I don't want to jinx it. As soon as I know for sure, you'll be the first to know."

"Fine." I roll my eyes.

Anna points at me. "You're not supposed to do that."

I can't help but laugh.

"It only counts when Nixon's around… I think…"

"Maybe I should text him," Anna teases.

"Sounds like a good time to me," I reply.

Anna giggles and shakes her head. "You're too much. I can't wait until we are back. FaceTime is great, but I miss spending real time with you."

"Me too, but it will be sooner than we know. You just kill that movie."

"I always do," she tells me with a wink.

I never thought I'd see the day that both Anna and I would be happy in relationships at the same time. But I admit, having her know about Nixon and being able to be open about it all is a breath of fresh air.

We say our goodbyes, end the call, and I take a moment to evaluate how I'm feeling.

I don't think I've ever felt this good. The only thing that's different in my life is Nixon.

Chapter 18

Nixon

THE RIBBING IMMEDIATELY BEGINS as soon as I pull a chair out at the table where my friends are sitting.

" 'Bout fucking time you showed up," Denver goads.

"Don't give him too hard of a time, or he'll leave," Bennett states, and I roll my eyes.

"You are all shitheads," I mutter with a smirk.

"You're the one who turned into a hermit," Knox adds.

"I'm not a hermit," I murmur, but I see why they think that.

I wish I could tell them why I've been bailing on beers with the guys, but I can't. I probably will never be able to. Sometimes that bothers me, but it's what I agreed to when Dante and I decided to try a real relationship.

"He isn't a hermit," Denver agrees. "Because I went by his house the other night to say hi, and he wasn't home." His eyes meet mine, and it almost breaks me.

"I have a life outside of work and my friendship with you assholes," I remind them.

Thankfully, the waitress chooses that moment to interrupt and take my drink order.

"I'll admit I've been a little MIA... so fill me in on what's new," I request after the waitress leaves, trying to get the attention off of me.

"My brother's best friend moved back a week ago," Knox says before taking a pull of his beer.

"The one you had the biggest crush on?" Bennett asks with wide eyes.

"Yup..." Knox admits on a sigh. "He's even hotter than he was when he left three years ago to serve with Doctors Without Borders."

"You gonna go for it this time?" I ask.

He shakes his head. "I can't. First off, my brother loves him more than me and would slit my throat. Second... I'm pretty sure he's straight."

"What do you mean *pretty sure?*' " Denver asks with a raised brow. "Aren't you either straight or not?"

I shrug. "Sexuality is like a spectrum. Some people lean more one way than the other. Others float around the middle. And sometimes, you think you lean one way, but something happens, and you start leaning the other way. It isn't always black and white."

Denver's brows pull together, and Bennett nods.

"I thought I was straight most of my life until a year ago when I realized I might be more pansexual... but labels are stupid, anyway," Bennett supplies, and Denver does a double take.

"Dude, you're almost forty, and you just figured out you aren't straight? Is that really possible?" Denver asks, and we all nod.

"Anything is possible. My dad is demisexual but had no idea until after my mom passed away. Then he started developing feelings for his best friend," Knox adds. "Now they are getting married next year. He's happy to be in a same-sex relationship but was sixty when he found that out."

Denver looks down at his beer, clearly mulling over the words, and I wonder what's going on in his head. I make a note to ask him after everyone leaves. No need to put him on the spot. If he wanted to talk about it with everyone here, he would.

"What about you, Bennett? Anything new?" I ask.

"Nope. Still single. My mom keeps pressuring me to date *anyone*. She keeps pulling the I'm-going-to-die-soon card. Which we all know is bullshit. She's not even sixty and is the healthiest person I know, but any emotional guilt trip she can take me on, she will," he says, shaking his head.

I chuckle because his mom is hilarious, and I can totally see her being all melodramatic.

We bullshit for a while, and I realize how much I missed these guys. As much as I *love* spending time with Dante, he's right. It's healthy for us to have a life outside of our relationship.

Bennett and Knox peace out first, leaving just Denver and me.

"Did you want to talk about something?" I ask after a minute of silence.

"When did you know you weren't straight?" he asks, keeping his eyes on his beer.

"I knew when I was ten, but that isn't the case for everyone. Are you questioning your sexuality?"

He shrugs. "I don't know. Maybe... I guess I'm just confused right now," he mutters.

"Well, I'm here if you ever want to talk."

He finally looks up and gives me a small smile. "Thanks, man. When I'm ready, I'll take you up on that."

"Take all the time you need... and don't beat yourself up. This is normal... even at thirty-five."

He chuckles and shakes his head. "At least I know I'm not alone. Knox's story about his dad helped a lot. Same with Bennett's."

"Good. I'm sure they'd be willing to talk to you too."

"I think I just have to get my head around what I'm feeling first."

"Makes perfect sense."

My phone buzzes, and it's a message from Dante that makes me smile.

"Do you have someone new in your life that you aren't telling us about?" Denver questions.

"It's new," I lie, hoping that will be enough for now.

"If he makes you smile like that, he must be special."

"He is," I say.

"I can't wait to meet him… when you're ready," Denver adds, and I have to force myself not to pull a face.

It's not about when *I'm* ready. It's about when Dante is ready, and that probably isn't ever.

"Sorry I stayed out longer than I said I would," I apologize as I strip before climbing into bed.

Dante cuddles into my side and rests his head on my chest.

"It's okay. Did you have a good time?"

"It was nice catching up again. Denver's going through some shit, which is why I didn't get away as fast as I originally planned."

"Is he okay?"

"I think so. Just confused about things he's feeling. I'm sure he'll figure it out, though."

"I like how much you care for your friends," Dante whispers, running his finger over my chest.

"It's hard lying to them, though," I admit.

Dante's body goes rigid, and I wish I could take the words back. It's not his fault that I'm feeling this way. He made it clear when we started this that he wouldn't be coming out anytime soon, and it's wrong of me to put these emotions on him.

"But I'll get through it," I add. "You make me really happy."

"You make me happy too," he whispers. "I love you."

Holy shit. I can't believe he said it first. I've been wanting to say those words for a while now, but I wasn't sure how he would take it.

"I love you too," I tell him as he tilts his head with a giant smile.

Leaning into him, I kiss him gently at first, before running my tongue along the seam of his lips and slipping into his mouth as soon as he gives me access. The kiss turns even more heated as Dante straddles me, rubbing our hard cocks together. My body feels like it's on fire with love and need for this boy.

Without saying a word, Dante grabs a condom and the lube, sheathing me before slicking up his hole quickly. Then he wastes no time lowering himself onto me and kissing me again.

A lot of our sex has been kinky, hard, and amazing, but this is different. This is passionate, slow, and sensual.

This isn't fucking...

... it's making love.

I let the sexy boy on top of me take control while I get my emotions in check and savor every second of our time together. I never want to forget this because it feels like something special for us.

"That's it, Treasure," I encourage him, breaking the kiss and starting to move a little faster. "Ride my cock."

"Fuck," he cries out as I reach down to stroke him, twisting my fist as I come up, making sure my grip is tight, the way I've learned he likes it.

"You're so fucking perfect." I buck my hips up, meeting him halfway.

Moans, gasps, and the sound of sex fills the room before Dante cries out one last time as his climax takes him over. His channel clamps so tight on my dick that I almost see spots as I find my release.

Dante collapses onto my chest, and I kiss the top of his head. "I love you," I tell him again.

"I love you," he repeats with a sleepy smile. "But I'm getting sticky from my cum," he adds, making me laugh. "Gah... I forgot how weird it is when you laugh while your dick is inside me."

"Come on. Let's have a quick shower. Then we can cuddle again."

Dante grumbles but carefully slides off me. Before he can get far, I grab his hand, still wanting physical contact as we head to the bathroom.

"Life has never been more perfect," Dante says with a giant smile before kissing me.

A twisting in my chest tells me I wish that statement were true.

Obviously, I'm so in love it hurts.

But I want more.

I'm just not allowed to ask for it.

Fuck, I hope this doesn't come to bite us in the ass.

Chapter 19

Dante

As soon as Brittany and Anna get off the private jet, I rush toward them. "Welcome back, bitches," I yell.

Anna runs directly into my arms, and I swing her around.

"Don't make my fiancée throw up," Brittany states. I stop and look into my best friend's eyes.

"Surprise," she yells, flashing the giant ring.

"Oh my God!" I gasp and pull her into my arms. "Congratulations, I'm so happy for you."

Last week, Anna went on a late-night show to talk about her sexuality and how being in the limelight can affect relationships. She left our relationship out of the conversation as much as possible, stating that we were best friends and I was helping her out by pretending to be her boyfriend. She went on to say she is in love and happier than ever.

When the interviewer started asking about babies, Anna broke down laughing. She and Brittany don't want kids and never have. It's something they talked about early on in their relationship.

Paparazzi have followed them since the announcement, but they knew that was coming. It's only going to get crazier for them now that they're engaged, but I don't think they care.

Thankfully, there hasn't been much talk about me except a few tabloids painting me to be some kind of saint, which almost makes me sick. I wasn't some selfless man staying single so my best friend could stay in the closet. But that's the way it's being portrayed.

Our management team is loving it, and I wonder if they had something to do with the narrative. As far as they know, it's true. I'm not planning on telling anyone ever again about my sexuality because, clearly, people can't be trusted.

"Are you sure you're fine with us living with you until we get our own place?" Anna asks, linking her arm in mine as we head toward Nixon's car, where he is waiting, keeping a close eye on all of us.

"Of course. It's *our* house and always will be. Stay as long as you want. You know how giant that place is. It's possible to go days without seeing someone if you really want to."

"I know. You did that once when you were pissed at me," Anna reminds me.

I laugh. "I don't even remember why I was mad."

She giggles and shakes her head. "Me either."

"This is weird," Anna states, cuddling with Brittany on one couch while Nixon and I are doing the same on another.

"What?" I ask as Nixon's fingers lazily play with the hem of my shirt.

"You, cuddling with a man and being in love," she teases.

I pick up a throw pillow and toss it at her. "It's not weird... it's nice." I stick my tongue out at her like the mature adult I am.

"Obviously, it's nice. I just never thought I'd see the day."

I look at Nixon and smile. "Me either, but I don't think I've ever been happier."

I move slightly and press my lips to his as Anna fakes a gagging noise.

"We need to get our own house so we don't have to see that all the time," Brittany jokes, cursing when a pillow hits her square in the face.

Nixon chuckles and kisses the top of my head.

"Nice toss," he praises, and I beam at him.

"This is your last week of filming, right?" Anna asks.

"Yup. It will be nice to have a tiny break."

Nixon's phone buzzes, and he excuses himself.

"Is Nixon going with you to Brazil to film the next movie?" Anna asks, and I bite my lip.

"We haven't really discussed that yet. It's still over two months away," I state, but that doesn't save me from a glare.

"You need to talk. It's a big deal. You'll be gone for six months," she reminds me like I was able to forget.

"I know. I don't see why he wouldn't come. His company is still my personal security. It makes sense to bring him along."

"Do you want him to go just because it makes sense?" Brittany asks.

"No. But I can't ask him to come along as *just* my boyfriend. We have to have a cover."

Brittany and Anna share a look but don't say anything else.

Thankfully, Nixon is back before the awkward silence settles in, but he looks a little off.

"Who was on the phone?" I ask when he sits beside me again.

"My mom," he says but doesn't add more. I don't pry even though I want to know why his smile isn't reaching his eyes.

My alarm goes off on my phone, letting me know it's bedtime, and I sigh.

"Only one week left of work." I groan as I stand. "See you guys tomorrow sometime," I tell Anna and Brittany before heading to bed.

"Is everything okay?" I ask Nixon when we are in our room.

"Yup, I just forgot my mom's birthday is next week."

"Oh yeah, moms hate when you forget shit like that," I reply as I strip out of my clothes.

"I also haven't been home for a visit in over six months, so she was guilt-tripping me hard."

"Mine doesn't even like me that much and still guilt-trips me occasionally. But I think it's just because she's trying to save my soul or something."

"My parents are actually pretty cool. Life has just gotten busy. But I think I am going to try and make it for her birthday, maybe even stay a week."

The idea of him being gone for a week feels weird, but I can't figure out why.

"I'm sure your parents will love that," I murmur as I climb into bed.

Nixon presses his lips together like he's stopping himself from saying something, but I don't know what. He stays silent as he strips, gets in behind me, and pulls me into his arms.

"I love you," he tells me, then kisses the top of my head, but his voice is full of emotion.

I want to ask what he's thinking about, but I'm scared of what he'll say.

"I love you too."

THE WEEK FLIES BY, and before I know it, I'm hugging my coworkers goodbye for now. We'll see each other soon enough on red carpets and press tours, but I get to not be *on* all the time for a while. It's an amazing feeling.

The only thing tampering with my joy is the fact that Nixon is leaving me tomorrow for a week. I'm going to miss him like crazy, and I still haven't brought up Brazil with him. He knows about me going, but it's like we are both avoiding talking about how it will work out.

"What time do you have to take off tomorrow?" I ask when we get home, thankful Anna and Brittany are out.

"Early. It's a ten-hour drive, and I don't want to get there too late," Nixon says, leaning against the island while I pour each of us a glass of water. "Would you like to come with me?" he asks, shocking me so much I drop my cup.

"Fuck," I curse and jump out of the way.

Nixon grabs a broom and sweeps up the shards of glass, but I barely move.

"Why would you want me to come with you?" I ask as Nixon empties the dustpan into the garbage can.

"To meet my parents," he replies. "I promise they won't say anything, but Mom is going to want to know who I've fallen for, and it would be nice to tell *someone*."

"I'm not ready," I bite out, turning to look out the window as anxiety washes over my body.

"I don't want to pressure you into doing anything, but it really sucks keeping this a secret sometimes."

My heart catches in my throat. I should have known this would happen. I'm an idiot for thinking this would work, for even *trying*.

"You knew I wasn't comfortable coming out when we entered this relationship," I remind him.

"I know..." He trails off, then takes a deep inhale. "I just didn't realize how hard it would be."

"If you don't want this, just say so," I tell him, turning to look at him.

"That's not what I meant," he assures me with kind eyes, but I shake my head.

"No… it's better if we end this now. Besides, I'm leaving for Brazil soon for six months. It would probably be best for me to have a different bodyguard so I can keep all my focus on my career… like I've always wanted to do." I'm fighting the tears that want to break free.

"Dante… don't do this," Nixon begs.

"We both knew this was never forever," I whisper, gazing at the floor.

"I'm sorry for bringing up my parents. I can make this work. Please don't break up with me. I love you."

"You should go now," I say, keeping my voice as even as possible.

Nixon doesn't listen and steps toward me, but I put my hand up, knowing I must do this. Not because I'm upset at him for inviting me to meet his parents or because he wants to tell people about us. No. The reason this has to end is because he deserves better. My fear will never let me come out, and Nixon deserves to be with someone he can boast about it.

"I love you," he repeats, and I squeeze my eyes shut.

"Please go," I plead, trying not to lose it.

"Is that what you really want?"

I nod, not trusting myself to say anything more.

"Give me ten minutes, and I'll be out of here."

I don't open my eyes, but Nixon's footsteps get quieter as he heads to my room to pack, and my heart shatters.

"I'll send over a list of bodyguards this week that I think would be a good fit for you for Brazil," Nixon says when he returns.

I give him a curt nod. I've barely moved except to turn and grip the countertop while staring outside. I'm afraid if I let go, I'll collapse, and I can't do that until Nixon is gone.

"If you need me, I'll be here," he tells me, but I can't respond. "And just to make it clear, I'm only leaving because you asked me to. I still love you."

The moment the door is shut behind him, I crumble to the floor, my body heaving with sobs.

Why can't I be strong enough for the man I love?

Why am I so fucked up in the head that I'd push him out the door instead of doing something so small?

Chapter 20

Dante

"Has he showered this week?"

"I don't think so. Should we just dump a bucket of soapy water on him?"

"It would ruin the couch."

"He can afford another one."

"*He* can hear you," I grumble from my spot on the couch, where I'm cocooned in a sea of blankets.

"Then *he* should get up, take a shower, and stop moping. You made your bed. Now you have to lie in it," Anna tells me firmly.

She was pissed when I told her what I did, but to this day, I still don't see another option. Nixon is an amazing man, and well... I'm me.

"I'm sick of this shit," Anna yells, stomping over to me and ripping the blankets off. "Get your ass in the fucking shower, then I'm driving you to a therapist."

"Hell fucking no," I scream.

"You need to talk to a professional. I should have forced this a long-ass time ago. Your family has fucked with your head so much that you are sabotaging your life. I refuse to watch you fall down this hole any longer."

"Then don't watch," I shout, my words dripping with venom.

Anna gasps, and the heartbroken look on her face does me in.

Sobs take over my body for the first time since Nixon left, and nausea rolls around in my stomach.

"I'm sorry," I whimper, gasping for air.

Warm arms surround me a second later, and Anna whispers calming words while I break down.

"Do you have a therapist you recommend?" I ask when I feel like I can breathe again.

"Brittany's sister. She's the best, and I promise she knows how to keep a secret."

I sigh. "This is going to fucking suck."

She helps me stand and says, "Probably at first, but it will be worth it... I promise."

At this point, I guess it's worth a shot.

WHILE I'M GETTING DRESSED, my phone rings, and I pause, staring at Elanor's name on my phone.

"You've got some nerve calling me," I answer.

"I'm sorry for everything, Dante... but I had to warn you..." She whimpers.

"Warn me about what? We already know you were trying to out me. I still don't know why, though. I thought we were friends."

"Your dad's been blackmailing me," she informs me.

I gasp. "What?"

"He somehow knows you're gay... I'm not the one who told him, I swear. He came to me a while ago wanting me to out you. Apparently, it would actually *help* his career because he can swing you leaving the church as to why you turned gay. He's also been looking for a reason to cut ties between you and your mother," she says, spilling the beans. "I played dumb at first, saying he was fed misinformation, but then he showed me a picture I didn't want out there, so I went along with his stupid plan. He's the one who hired the creepy guy on the red carpet to drug you. I was told it was only supposed to loosen your lips, but part of me wonders if your dad actually wanted you dead. I know I wronged you, but I want to make it right now."

"What about the break-in?" Now is the time to get answers.

"You were supposed to be at an event. He hired people to ransack your house. Figured you had to have something in there that would prove you were gay."

"Why should I believe you?"

"Because he's done waiting. I wasn't producing proof fast enough, and he fired me. I don't know what he's going to do, but I don't think it's going to be good. I'm not a fool to think we can mend bridges... but I wanted to give you a heads-up that something bad is coming, and you might want to get ahead of it now."

"Don't call me again," I snap and end the call.

How do I know what she's saying is truthful and isn't her just trying one more time to get me to out myself?

My head races as I finish getting dressed and meet Anna by the front door.

"You're white as a ghost," she states.

"Elanor just called," I whisper, still trying to sort out my thoughts.

Anna's eyes go wide, and she gasps.

"What did that bitch have to say?"

"I'll tell you on the drive." I open the front door and am about to make my way to her car when I see Denver standing there.

"What's he doing here?" I ask Anna.

"I wasn't sure if you were supposed to leave the house by yourself, so I called Nixon," she admits.

"Fuck it." I shrug and get into the back of the SUV with Anna beside me.

"So what did Elanor have to say?" Anna asks as Denver drives us to the therapist.

I don't respond right away, knowing that if I tell Anna now, Denver will know I'm gay, but if Elanor was telling the truth, the whole world is going to find out sooner rather than later. Why not start by telling someone Nixon trusted more than anyone else?

Taking a deep breath, I close my eyes and try to center myself before looking at Denver.

"You're good at keeping secrets, right?"

"The best," he replies.

"Well, buckle up. I'm about to drop a bunch of truth bombs, and you'll need to keep your mouth shut, even from Nixon."

Denver growls, and his jaw tenses.

"Nixon is my friend. I don't like keeping shit from him," he says.

"You two are a lot alike," I state. "I'm not asking you to keep it forever, just until I can figure out how to tell him... okay?"

He sighs but nods. "Fine... I'll keep my mouth shut, but not forever. If you don't tell him on your own in one month, I will."

I don't argue with the timeline. It's better than I would have thought.

With that, I tell them both about my conversation with Elanor.

"Shit." Anna has about the same reaction I did.

"I'm not sure I believe her... but I also don't put this past my dad either." I blow out a breath and cast my eyes toward Denver.

"Any questions?" I ask him.

"Are you the guy Nixon's in love with?"

Damn. I knew the man was good, but he picked up on that quickly.

"I was... I kind of broke up with Nixon last week just before he left to visit his parents."

"Why the hell would you do a thing like that?" he bites out.

"Because I need help," I admit.

"And he's getting it," Anna adds, jumping in.

Denver nods, keeping his eyes on the road.

"Nixon's a good man, and the last thing I want is to see him broken... but the way he smiled at his phone on guys' night tells me that you mean a lot to him. So hurry up and get that help so you can fix your relationship. Everyone deserves to be happy."

His words hit me right in the heart, and a few tears slide down my face.

"I'm trying."

"Good afternoon, Dante. I'm Dr. Melissa Riser, but you can just call me Mel." Brittany's sister greets me with a warm smile.

"Thanks for fitting me in." I reach out to shake her hand.

"Well, Brittany was very adamant that this was an emergency, and I had a last-minute cancellation, so it worked out well."

I nod and sit on the comfy couch across from a chair she sits in.

"What would you like to talk about today?"

"How do I stop fear from ruling my life?" I ask, not wanting to say everything quite yet.

"That's a complicated question to answer," she replies. "First, we have to figure out what that fear stems from. What are you afraid of?"

"I don't even know anymore. I thought I was afraid of the world knowing I'm gay… and I think that's still true… but it's almost more than that. I've lived in the closet for so long with no desire to come out, but that decision is most likely being taken away from me soon." I take a deep breath before I can continue. "Also… I've fallen in love, and it isn't fair to him that we have to be a secret. But even if it meant keeping him, it's like my body won't let me shout it from the rooftops. I should *want* to come out for him. I love him with all my heart… but it's like I'm physically incapable of doing it. So instead, I pushed him out of my life."

Mel nods as she writes a few things down. "What kind of upbringing did you have?" she asks gently.

"My dad is a pastor of a mega-church. He's also running for office. Obviously, very conservative and pretty much a giant asshole. We don't really have a relationship, but that doesn't bother me. My mother only had me because she was supposed to. I don't think she ever really loved or wanted me. I figured out I was gay pretty early on but didn't say anything because I'm certain they would have tried to send me to conversion therapy. Anna and I met on day one of kindergarten and were instant best friends. She was the first person I told, and she didn't even bat an eye. Just told me it didn't matter. I knew that wasn't really true, though. It does matter… to some people."

"So your parents don't know you're gay?"

I shrug. "I guess my dad knows and is apparently trying to out me. I just found that out today."

"Wow," Mel whispers.

"My other best friend from high school claims my dad was blackmailing her. I'm not really sure if I should believe her… but honestly, I don't put it past him."

"That's a lot to be dealing with."

"I just want to be done with all of this."

"Religious trauma is something a lot of people deal with, and it sounds like that is the main culprit of your fear. You were raised to believe that being gay is wrong, and even though you don't think that, there is a part of your brain that still does. I believe that's why you panic when you think about coming out."

I rest my head against the back of the couch and sigh. "So how do I get past this, then?" I *need* to know the answer.

"Therapy," she replies with a cheeky grin, looking so much like her sister. "I can teach you coping mechanisms to almost override the negative thoughts. It's not going to be easy, and it's going to require a lot of work from you, but it's possible to get through this. I've seen a lot of people overcome religious trauma."

"I'll do whatever it takes."

I'm done letting this fear control me. So many times over the years, I've wanted to say fuck my parents and come out of the closet, but I could never go through with it. Maybe Mel can help me get past this barrier.

Chapter 21

Nixon

DENVER TAKES A SIP of his coffee, fidgeting in the chair on the other side of my desk. "Are you sure you want me to go with Dante to Brazil?" he asks.

Leaning back, I stare him down. He's not telling me something, but I don't know what.

"You've been wanting a full-time client for a long-ass time. Why aren't you jumping for joy? Did you change your mind?"

He shakes his head. "Nah, man, I still want a full-time client. I just think you should be the one going with him. You've been his bodyguard since day one. Why the change?"

My jaw hurts from how hard I'm grinding my teeth as I stare out the window. I wish I could tell him everything. Denver is one of my closest friends, but I won't ever betray Dante's trust.

"You guys got along well while I was at my parents' house. And I think it would be best if I don't leave the country for months. I have to run this business. You're perfect for this job, but if you want me to give it to someone else, I will. Bennett would probably be all for it."

The mention of my trip to see my parents takes me back.

"You made it," Mom shouts with a giant smile that falls from her face when her eyes land on mine. "What's wrong?"

I shake my head and pull her into my arms. For the first time since Dante ripped my heart from my chest, I cry like a fucking baby while my mom holds me and rubs my back. She whispers promises that everything is going to be all right, but no one can know that.

When I left Dante's house to see them, I left something behind. My heart. He holds it, and I'm not sure if I'm ever going to feel whole again. Not unless he takes me back, which I don't see happening.

Denver huffs out a breath and shakes his head, pulling me to the present again.

"Is there something you want to add?" I inquire, noticing his tight jaw and how agitated he looks.

"I guess not. But maybe you should call *him* and make sure he's good with the change." Denver is a bit on edge when he leaves my office, and his tone has me tilting my head as I watch him close my door.

Hmm...

But I don't have the energy to decipher what's going on with him, so I check my emails and schedule people where they need to be. It's like I'm running on autopilot.

Everything feels so fucking wrong. I knew this heartbreak was inevitable. I tried to prepare myself, but I had no idea how bad this would hurt.

Is this emptiness ever going to go away?

I fell in love with Dante Michaelson. He might have been the one to break things off, but I'm the only one to blame for this pain. I knew where he stood from day one. He never lied to me.

This was always how things were supposed to go.

IT'S BEEN THREE WEEKS since I've seen Dante, and each day that passes feels the same. It's like I'm moving through a fog. Nothing I do lifts it. I'm living in a world of gray, and I want the color back.

I text Anna every day, making sure he's okay, and Denver has been on call for when Dante leaves the house, so I know he's fine, but it's not the same.

I miss him so fucking much, but there isn't anything I can do. The thing is, I get why he pushed me out. He's scared, but it doesn't make it hurt any less.

Anna told me he's working on things, but I won't hold my breath. Hope is a dangerous thing.

Glancing at my phone, I blow out a breath and fight the urge to text Dante. To call him. To have any form of communication with him. I could use work as a guise, but I know the moment I hear his voice, it will be my undoing.

The numbness in my veins is better than the pain I felt that first week. I don't know if I can survive that a second time.

Needing a distraction, I leave my phone on the desk, grab a bag, and head to the office gym. "I'm heading for a workout if anyone is looking for me," I tell Margret, our receptionist, as I pass her desk.

"Sounds good," she says with a smile that lights up her face.

I dip my chin in her direction and walk away, unable to return the cheery look.

MY ARMS BURN AS I push the bar for my chest press, shaking as I struggle to put it back in place. I know better than to bench this much weight without a spotter, but I wanted to *feel* something.

"Are you an idiot?" Denver shouts as he rushes over, helping me put the bar on the rack above my head.

My breathing is heavy as I sit up and reach for my water bottle. "I was fine," I grumble before guzzling the cold liquid.

"You could seriously hurt yourself benching that much without someone here."

I feel like shit because I know that.

Maybe I was trying to hurt myself.

"What's going on with you? You haven't been acting like yourself since you got back from your trip, which you extended... also not like you."

"It's nothing," I lie, my heart still racing from how hard I was pushing my body.

Denver glares at me, gritting his teeth. "I'm surprised your eyes aren't brown from the bullshit you're spewing right now."

"It's personal," I respond as honestly as I can.

"And I thought we were friends." He looks at the floor.

"It's not just my story to tell, okay?"

He presses his lips together as if wondering how much he should push me, but after a moment of intense eye contact, he only nods. I guess he decided it wasn't worth the fight today, and I'm thankful for that because I don't think it would take much for me to crack.

"I'm here if you need to talk," Denver says after a heavy silence.

"I appreciate the offer, man." I dip my chin. "What brought you in here, anyway?" I ask as I stand to pack up my shit, my workout officially done.

"I went to your office to ask you about the red-carpet event this weekend for Dante, and Margret told me where to find you."

Shit, I almost forgot about that event. I've been so tied up in everything else that it slipped my mind. "Meet me in my office in thirty, and we'll go over everything," I state, then head to the bathroom for a quick shower.

Everything inside me is screaming for me to be at the event with my guys to keep my eyes on Dante and guarantee nothing happens to him, but I'm not sure that is a good idea.

Would he even want me there?

Probably not.

After my shower, I head to my office and find Denver and Bennett already there. "Hey, guys, ready to go over everything?" I ask, and they nod, ready to get to work.

I need to treat this like I would any other client. My guys are more than qualified to keep Dante safe. That will have to be good enough.

The meeting with my guys goes by quickly, and we come up with a solid plan to address any potential concerns and do our best to keep him safe. Yet something in my stomach isn't sitting right. I want to trust my gut, but it's hard to when I'm pretty sure my feelings are the ones causing this unease.

Once our talk is over, it's quitting time. I take the long way to my house, not in any rush to get home. I miss living with Dante. Miss how noisy and obnoxious he could be. Miss the way he would curl into me when we watched a movie or fell asleep. He loved to touch and be touched, and now that I'm living on my own again, my body feels cold. My house is too fucking quiet. I miss having someone to talk to and hold.

Everything is just so bland.

I wish things were different.

AT ELEVEN, I FINALLY turn off the television and *try* to sleep. Something that hasn't been easy since the breakup. How could such a short amount of time with someone change so much in how I find comfort?

Before Dante, I used to love being by myself. Never had an issue sleeping. I was so content with life. Now I hate the quiet and miss the feel of a body pressed against mine. I miss the man I love.

How long does it take to get over these feelings?

As I pull back the covers, my phone blares, and I rush to it, recognizing the familiar tone I set for Dante's security system. My heart plummets as I watch the cameras and see a masked man enter the property.

Working on autopilot, I send a mass text to my team, informing them about what is happening. Denver and Bennett agree to meet me at Dante's house, and Sophy calls the police while keeping an eye on the cameras. I rush to get to my car and drive like a bat out of hell to the house of the most important person in the world to me. *He can't be hurt. I can't let him down.*

I call Dante's cell, but he doesn't answer, which doesn't surprise me. Still, it irritates me. After getting sent to voicemail, I call Anna and pray she is there.

"Hello?" Anna answers in a sleepy voice.

"Are you at Dante's house?" I question, taking a sharp left turn.

"Yeah... what's going on?"

"Did you not get a notification that someone is on the property?"

She gasps but doesn't respond right away. When she comes back, she says, "The system didn't alert us. What should we do?"

"Get Dante and get to the safe room. I'm on my way, and so are the cops. Don't come out until you hear my code."

She doesn't respond, but she's talking to someone, probably Brittany, letting her know about the situation. It feels like forever before she talks to me again, letting me know they are all safe.

As soon as I have that confirmation, I end the call, and not long after, I pull into Dante's driveway. Denver and Bennett show up behind me, so I let us all through the gate.

"Search the property," I instruct the guys as we exit our vehicles. "I'm heading to make sure everyone in the house is okay." They nod and head off in opposite directions.

I make my way to the safe room we had installed after the first break-in. Three knocks and a shout of "*Pineapple doesn't belong on pizza*" has the door opening, and I'm face to face with three terrified people in pajamas.

My eyes beeline for Dante.

"Are you okay?" I ask everyone, but my eyes don't leave the handsome actor.

Dante nods before casting a glance at Anna.

"We need to talk," he says once his eyes are on mine again.

"The property is clear," Bennett yells.

"Two seconds," I tell Dante before turning and walking toward Denver and Bennett. "They left?" I question my guys, who nod.

"The cops got here as the person was running away. They went after him, and we did a second sweep of the property just to be certain," Denver supplies. "I'm not sure what he was planning on doing, but he's gone."

A tap on my shoulder has me turning to see hazel eyes that I haven't been able to stop thinking about. "Can we talk?" Dante asks with a hint of urgency, and I nod and follow him to the living room.

What could he possibly want now? He's already ripped my heart out.

As soon as we are alone, he crashes into me, squeezing me so tight it's almost hard to breathe. I return the hug, loving how Dante feels in my arms but also dreading the fact that I'll eventually have to let go.

"Thank you for coming to my rescue," he whispers, still clinging to me.

I drop a kiss to the top of his head, letting my lips rest there for a minute. "I promised I would never let anyone hurt you. I'll never break that vow."

He pulls away the slightest amount so he can stare up into my eyes. The urge to kiss him is so strong, but I won't be the one to make the first move here. Pushing up onto his toes, his lips land on mine, and I melt into his mouth.

The kiss is slow and delicate, and I wish it would last forever, but there are so many things we need to talk about first.

"I've missed you," I whisper against his lips, needing to pull away. His lips and mouth are too easy to get lost in, and I need to maintain some clarity. Too many things need to be said, and my heart can't take any more hurt.

"I'm sorry I pushed you away," he responds with sad eyes. "I'm also sorry for keeping a secret."

"Let's sit." I guide him to the couch, shoving down any hope that we might get back together.

"Elanor called me about a week after we broke up. It was the day I started therapy," he explains, and even though I'm pissed that she called, I don't interrupt. Dante needs to finish his story. "She informed me that my dad was blackmailing her. He wants to out me for his political career. She was just trying to protect herself. I still don't think I can forgive her, but I get it. Apparently, she wasn't giving him proof fast enough, so he fired her."

Movement outside catches my attention, and I see a figure rushing away.

"I thought you said he left," I yell, gaining Denver and Bennett's attention as I rush outside.

I run as fast as my legs will carry me, but I'm not fast enough. By the time I reach the edge of the property, the guy is getting into a black Ford Escape with no license plates and making his getaway.

"Fuck," I scream at the top of my lungs, pulling out my phone and heading back to the house.

"How come I wasn't aware there was more than one person on the property?" I complain the second Sophy answers.

"I didn't know," she shouts in response. "Something is fucked up with the system. As soon as the first guy left the property, the cameras went on a loop, and I didn't clue in until a few minutes ago. Whoever hacked the system is a fucking expert and left very few footprints. I doubt I'll be able to trace this to anyone."

"I have an idea of who hired the person," I grumble, stepping into the house. "See what you can find. In the meantime, we'll move Dante to a more secure location."

"On it," she says and ends the call.

"Dante, can we talk privately?" I request with a tip of my head.

He quietly follows me to his bedroom, and I shut the door behind us.

"If what you just told me is true, I think your father planned tonight. And there is a strong chance they have footage of us kissing."

Dante's eyes go wide and glassy with unshed tears as he shakes his head.

"What do you want to do?" I ask, reaching for his hands. "I'll do whatever you want. Just tell me what to do."

"I don't know," he whispers before pulling me in and resting his head on my chest.

I rub his back as he cries into my chest, wishing things were different. "I'm sorry this is happening. I'm sorry we didn't get ahead of this," I whisper.

"I'm the one who should be sorry," he murmurs.

We don't say anything as we hold onto one another. It's like we both need each other's strength.

A knock on our door breaks the moment, and I take a step away, clearing my throat that's threatening to clog with unshed tears.

Hope was bubbling to the surface, and in his embrace, I was teetering on giving in. Dante is within arms' reach but still too far away.

How do we close this gap?

"I just wanted to check on you," Anna says after Dante opens the door.

"I'm scared," he confesses to her.

"It's okay. You're going to get through this," Anna assures him, wrapping her arms tightly around him.

I hate that I'm not the one holding him anymore.

"We need to figure out what we are going to do now," I say after a moment. "It would be easier if my team knew exactly what we are up against, but I understand if you still want to keep your secret."

"Denver already knows," Dante responds. "I told him when he took me and Anna to my therapist appointment." I grind my teeth, pissed that Denver didn't tell me, but Dante quickly puts an end to my anger. "I made him promise not to tell you anything, so don't get mad at him. I'm still trying to fix myself, but I promise I'm getting better. You can tell whoever you think needs to know. If you trust them, so do I." He takes a deep breath, and my eyes go wide, but I nod.

"Come on, let's go sit with the others, and I'll call Sophy too."

I'm not sure what will happen after tonight, but I can't let my hopes get too high. All I know is I'm happy Dante is working on himself. Even if we can't be together, he deserves to be happy.

Chapter 22
Dante

NIXON GOES OVER THE basics of everything that has happened up until tonight with his team before turning his attention to Anna, Brittany, and me. "It's probably best that you all stay somewhere else tonight," he says.

"Why? We know no one is trying to hurt me. My dad just wants to out me. Now he has the proof to do it, so what's the point in running?" I ask, feeling deflated.

"I feel like I failed you," Sophy states through Nixon's phone sitting on the coffee table on speaker. "It's my job to make sure your system doesn't get hacked, and I fucked it up."

"My father has a lot of money, Sophy. When he has his heart set on something, he'll use whatever he can to get his way. I know how amazing you are. This isn't your fault," I say, trying to reassure her.

"What's the game plan, then? Do we still need to be here?" Denver asks.

"Our main job stays the same, keep our client safe, but I'm not going to lie and say I don't want to pin all of this shit on Dante's father and ruin his political career," Nixon grumbles.

"Now that I have a name and some background information, I might be able to help with that," Sophy pipes up, and even though these people are trying to help me, it still feels pointless.

"I'm going to call my PR team in the morning and go public about my sexuality as soon as possible," I tell everyone. They all stare at me intensely. "There's no avoiding this anymore. I can wait for my father to release the photos I'm sure were taken tonight, or I can step out in front of it. Either way, he gets what he wants. At least this way, I can keep Nixon out of the limelight."

"You don't need to protect me," Nixon tells me with a determined look on his face, bringing a small smile to mine.

"This time I do," I counter softly.

"Do you think we should double up security for tomorrow's late-night talk show appearance?" Denver asks. "Just in case this gets leaked beforehand."

"Not a bad idea," Nixon agrees.

"Maybe we should also go over the details for the red-carpet event while we are all here," Denver adds.

"It might be more chaotic than normal if I'm coming out before then," I remind them.

"Bennett and I will be by your side the entire time," Denver assures me, but I look at Nixon.

"Aren't you going to be there?" I ask.

"I wasn't sure you wanted me there."

I nod, unsure of what to say. I know I fucked up. I wish I had a time machine to go back and erase it all, but that isn't possible.

I've been seeing Mel every other day for the past few weeks. She's helping me clear out the hurt caused by my parents and deal with my anxiety. I knew my head was a messed-up place but didn't realize how bad it had gotten. For the first time in… well, maybe ever… I feel like a light is at the end of the tunnel. While I'm still terrified to come out, it isn't as crippling as it would have been a month ago.

"Should we have someone stay on the property for the next week or so to ensure there isn't some sort of backlash from Dante's coming out?" Bennett asks.

"That's a good idea. I'll stay for tonight. Tomorrow, we can come up with a rotating schedule," Nixon replies. "If that's okay with you," he adds, staring into my eyes.

"That works. We should probably talk, anyway," I say.

Nixon nods before turning his attention back to his team. "Sophy, you keep working on linking Arnold Michaelson to Dante's stalking, harassment, and attempted murder. Denver, Bennett... you two do a final sweep of the property before leaving just to make sure no one is left snooping around. Tomorrow, we can regroup and go over a more thorough plan once Dante's PR team figures out how they want to handle the situation."

Everyone agrees, and Nixon ends the call with Sophy while Denver and Bennett let themselves out. Anna and Brittany tell us goodnight before heading to bed, leaving Nixon and me alone.

"Are you sure you want to go through with this plan?" Nixon asks after a few moments of silence.

"This isn't just about protecting you. It's about wanting to lead my own narrative for once. Through therapy, I discovered my parents fucked me up much worse than I thought. I distanced myself, but I let their misguided love control me. That's why I never made statements when my father would talk about me leaving the faith, why I made sure I had a girlfriend, even if it was a fake relationship, and why I never came out. All because I wanted to make people who should love me no matter what proud. I'm done with that. I like who I am, and I like me better when I'm with you. I know I fucked this all up, but if you'll give me a second chance, I promise I'll make it up to you," I say through watery eyes and a thickness in my throat.

Nixon pulls me into his arms and holds me. "I can't do this closet thing anymore. I thought I could, but I can't," he whispers, pulling away to look into my eyes. "I want to shout how much I love you from the rooftops. So if you're certain about coming out and continuing to work on your mental health, then I'm all yours."

"It's not always going to be easy for me," I admit, but the smile he offers me in return settles my nerves.

"Nothing worthwhile is ever easy," Nixon replies, then leans in and brushes his lips against mine. "But I'm willing to put in the work if you are."

"I love you," I tell him before grabbing the back of his neck and pulling him back for a passionate kiss.

"Fuck, I missed this," he whispers, breaking this kiss for only a moment.

"Take me to bed," I command, and Nixon chuckles in a deep, sexy tone.

"Gladly."

"Do you want to be a part of my coming-out story?" I ask Nixon as he drives us to my PR firm's office.

"Do *you* want me to be?"

I stare out the window at the passing buildings, thinking about my response. "You said you don't want to be a dirty secret, but you also didn't necessarily sign up for all the bullshit that comes with dating a celebrity."

Nixon keeps his left hand on the steering wheel, places his other on my knee, and squeezes. "Babe, I can handle myself. I know what I'm signing up for. I love you, and I'll take whatever gets thrown at us. I wish you didn't have to do this on such a big scale, so if you want to share that with me, I'm here."

Letting out a contented sigh, I smile at him. "How are you so perfect?"

He chuckles. "I'm far from perfect... but you're stuck with me."

I love the idea of being with Nixon for the rest of my life. I never questioned my love for Nixon once it began to feel right. And that confused me because if I was so happy and in love, why didn't I want to shout it from the rooftops? Instead, I wanted to stay in our happy bubble of solitude. I struggled with that a lot when I first started therapy. Apparently, it boils down to my upbringing. My parents were very much don't-ask-don't-tell people about *everything*. Was it really a sin if someone didn't know you were sinning?

So, in the comfort of my own home, my life with Nixon was perfect, and I was truly fucking happy. It was telling anyone about it that freaked me the fuck out. Because that's when it becomes real. That's when shit hits the fan. That's when the panic set in, and I pushed Nixon out.

I hate that my parents are the ones who fucked up my head, and at the same time, my father is the one pushing me out of the closet. He's the reason I've lived in it for so long and never wanted to leave. Pretty ironic if you think about it.

Pulling into the parking lot, Nixon gets out and opens the passenger door for me. "I'm here for you in whatever way you need me," he promises, balling his fists at his sides.

He's probably itching to touch me but respects me enough not to do it publicly. At least not until I'm comfortable with it, which is *not* today, although I am craving his warmth and strength. *Maybe I should have gotten my team to meet me at my house.*

It's too late for that, so I force my feet to move and head into the building, Nixon directly behind me. I may not be able to touch him in public yet, but thankfully, his closeness brings me a sense of calm.

"Right this way, Mr. Michaelson," a young blonde at the front desk says with a tilt of her head.

We follow her to a board room, where my team is already set up.

"It's great to see you, Dante," Amara, my new manager, says with a bright smile as she shakes my hand.

"I wish this was under better circumstances," I reply.

"Of course. Why don't you sit, and we can get to work," she suggests.

Nixon pulls out my chair for me, and I give him a thankful smile before sitting across from the team.

"So your message this morning was a little ominous, but we are ready for whatever curveball you throw at us." Amara's eyes are filled with kindness, and it makes me want to trust her, even though that has never been something I've been good at. Another thing I can thank my parents for.

"I thought it would be better if I explained in person, but I want to start by thanking you for meeting with me on such short notice," I begin, hoping I can get this out easily. "As you know, I was drugged at an event a while ago and could have easily died. Unfortunately, some new information has turned up, and I'm at a crossroad. We know my old manager was partly responsible for the situation. What we recently found out is that she was being blackmailed by my father..."

I pause, taking in the team's shocked faces.

"I wasn't entirely honest with you when we signed our contract, and I hope you can forgive me for that... I told you my manager was trying to get me to spill personal information about myself, but

I didn't say what that information was..." I pause again, my throat thickening with nerves, making it hard to swallow.

"That isn't being dishonest, Dante. Everyone is entitled to keep information to themselves. You don't owe us anything. We are here to best support you, but if you don't want to share things with us, that is your right," Amara assures me.

"Thank you, that means a lot, but I do have to tell you the secret now because it's about to get leaked," I inform them. "Last night, my security system was hacked, and intruders made their way onto my property. Nixon and his team were quick to arrive and make sure the situation was handled. Unfortunately, since the system was hacked, we were unaware that there were two intruders, not just one. Thinking the coast was clear, I kissed Nixon, and we are pretty sure the second person took photos. The hacker was someone who knew what he was doing, which screams expensive, making me think my father was connected. Since he now most likely has photo evidence of my sexuality, it won't be long before the world knows. I want to get ahead of this and tell the world myself. Maybe that way, my father won't release the images, but I can't guarantee that either."

The team is silent after I finish, but Amara has the same warm smile, with only the tiniest bit of sadness behind her eyes.

"I can't believe your father is doing this," she says with clear disgust in her voice. "What does he have to gain from you coming out?"

"He's moved into politics recently. According to Elanor, he thinks it will help his rankings. Honestly, I can see it. He'll be able to say the reason I'm gay is because I left the church or some bullshit story."

"I've seen things like this before," Rayleen, my PR rep says. "I hate that you have to go through this, but there are a ton of ways we can get ahead of the story."

"Can we bring his dad down in the process?" a guy sitting next to Rayleen grumbles.

"We're working on that," Nixon says. "So far, we have no way of actually tying him to the events. But if we can nail him, we will."

"Are you two dating?" Amara asks. "You can tell me to shut up if you want. I just want to have as much information as possible, but I'll never push you outside of what you're comfortable with."

I turn to Nixon, wondering what I should say. We talked briefly before we ended up in bed together, but we didn't go through what being together actually looks like. Throwing caution to the wind, I turn my attention to my team again. "We are, but I don't want that out for the public yet," I tell them.

"We can make that work," Rayleen assures me with a smile. "You are supposed to be on one of the new live late-night talk shows tonight. Would you like to make the announcement then? I'm sure the host would love to be the one who gets to broadcast that."

Fuck. I know I said I wanted to do this soon, but tonight is so fast. However, I don't see my father holding on to his newfound information for too long.

"Okay, is there a way to have him prepared for my announcement without telling him beforehand?" I question, not trusting anyone to not run with this and leak it early.

"Absolutely, we'll just let the producers know you have something special you want to tell the world. They'll eat it up, I'm sure," Amara promises me.

It doesn't entirely settle my nerves, but at least it's a plan.

"I'll have two extra bodyguards with me tonight for after the show in case things get hectic," Nixon tells the team. "Our job is to make sure Dante stays safe. We intend to do that."

"Sounds perfect. I'll make sure to get you all passes," Amara says with a smile.

"Do you want me to write up a script for you?" Rayleen asks.

I shake my head. "I want it to come from the heart. I think that will go over better with my fans."

"I agree. I'm sure you are aware that you are going to receive some level of hate," Amara informs me, and I nod. "But I also think you will receive a lot of love. We won't let this ruin your career."

"Thank you all so much," I tell them and push back my chair. "Fingers crossed tonight goes well."

Amara stands with me, coming around the table to place her hand on my shoulder. "We've got you. I'll see you tonight. Try not to freak out too much before then."

"Easier said than done," I grumble, leaving with Nixon.

"Denver and Bennett are meeting us at your house," Nixon tells me as soon as we get into the car.

"Are you still planning on working out a rotating schedule?" I ask, hoping that isn't the plan.

"Do you want someone else with you at night?" he questions with a smirk.

I playfully shove his shoulder. "Of course not. I just wasn't sure where we stood. I know I told my team we're dating, but you and I haven't fully discussed that..." I trail off and run my fingers through my hair.

I've been letting it grow out since the ending of the last movie, and I like that I have something to play with.

"I'm yours, Dante," he states firmly, and now there isn't a doubt in my mind that he means it.

"Maybe we should figure out a plan on moving you in permanently, then," I suggest.

Nixon smiles brightly. "I'd love that."

"ARE YOU SURE YOU don't want me there for moral support?" Anna asks, biting her lip.

"I want you to stay here and be safe. You've already dealt with so much during our fake relationship. Who knows how tonight is going to turn out? Obviously, Nixon and the guys will keep me safe, but I don't want you involved in this."

Her pout is almost enough to make me cave.

"I'll be watching and cheering you on from home." Anna pulls me in for a hug. "I'm so proud of you," she whispers into my ear, and I squeeze her a little tighter.

"Come on, Amara, Bennett and Denver are waiting for us," Nixon says, tilting his head toward the door.

I blow out a breath before following my man to the car. I still can't believe I'm doing this. My heart is racing, and my chest feels tight, all of which is apparently normal, but I hate it. Thankfully, I had a call with Mel earlier, and she walked me through a few techniques to use tonight if things get too hard.

Everyone keeps telling me they're so proud of me. It's weird because I don't think I ever heard those words growing up. In my parents' eyes, I could never do anything right. Maybe that makes this a tiny bit easier. I'll never make them happy, and they will always spin things to suit them. They don't love me, and that's okay because I have people in my life who actually give a damn, and they are the ones in my corner tonight.

Arriving at the studio, I take a deep breath. Tonight, everything changes for me. And while I'm terrified, I'm also excited and thankful.

As soon as I step out of the closet, I'll finally be free. That's if my fear doesn't pull me under to drown me before then.

Chapter 23

Nixon

ANXIETY RADIATES OFF DANTE as we make our way to the green room. I wish I could take that away from him. My hands itch to touch him and pull him into my arms, but I can't do that yet.

"Everything is all set," Amara informs Dante with a giant smile. "Eric will start the interview talking about the movie and will segue into your important announcement shortly after that."

Dante nods, wringing his hands in front of him. His face is pale, and he looks like he's about to throw up.

"You can change your mind," I remind him, but he shakes his head.

"I... I can do this."

"You can... but sometimes it's nice to have people in your corner," a petite woman with fiery red hair and piercing green eyes says with a grin.

Denver is standing behind her, giving me a nod before walking away, heading back to where he is to be positioned.

"Mel?" Dante squeaks. "What are you doing here?" he asks, rushing to pull her in for a hug.

"Brittany told me you refused to let her and Anna be here. I knew it would be important for you to have a shoulder you could lean on..." she pauses to look at me and winks, "... besides your super handsome boyfriend."

"You aren't what I was expecting," I remark, reaching out my hand.

She shakes it and shrugs. "I'm normally more professional, but Dante and I have grown close. The lines have kind of blurred since he's so close to my sister, and we've hung out a few times outside of the office," she tells me. Then, to Dante, she says, "Keep taking deep breaths. Remember, it's okay to pause and focus on yourself during the interview. What you are doing isn't an easy thing. If the host tries to push you to speak faster than you are ready to, I'll send your bodyguard boyfriend out to kick his ass."

Mel teasing Dante makes his lips tip up and brings a little color to his face.

"You're on in five minutes," a producer tells Dante, sticking his head into the room.

"Let's do a quick breathing exercise." Mel holds his hands.

She coaches him through deep inhales through his nose and long exhales through his mouth. I love that she's able to calm him like this. I wish I could be more help, though. I feel so useless right now. Dante is my boyfriend. I should be the one who can get him to relax and ease his worries. But right now, I'm one of his triggers. The only thing I can do is be here and do my best to keep the outside world from hurting him.

"Time to go," Amara states.

We all make our way to the stage and wait for further instructions. It doesn't take long, and a producer walks Dante closer to the curtain, and within seconds, the host invites him onto the stage as the room erupts with applause.

Dante waves, smiles, and looks at ease, but I can tell it's a front—one he has mastered over the years. He's a talented actor, so it's easy for him to convince people he's fine when that isn't always the case.

I keep my eyes on my man the entire time, knowing my team is watching our surroundings.

"Dante, you have killed it again. People are already raving about your newest movie, and it's not even out yet," Eric O'Connor says with a charming smile.

"Thanks, Eric. It was a fun movie to film. I know every superhero lover is going to enjoy it once it's out," Dante replies with an easy demeanor.

They move on to talk about the filming process and the hardest part about being an action star before Eric reveals a surprise to the audience.

"We actually have a sneak peek trailer for our audience. What do you say... should we share it?" Eric asks Dante.

"Absolutely," my man agrees and leans back in his chair as the lights dim and large screens slide down before projectors start the movie trailer.

Eric leans into Dante, and I wish I could hear what he's saying. Thankfully, my man doesn't tense at the words being spoken. He looks like whatever Eric is telling him is putting him at ease. The smile he gives the host is genuine, and it almost makes me jealous.

I don't realize how hard I'm grinding my molars until a warm hand touches my arm, and I release.

"How are you doing?" Mel whispers.

"I'm not the one about to make a giant announcement," I respond.

"True... but this is still something huge for you. I'm sure you have some feelings around all of this."

"I wish I could be the one who puts him at ease," I tell her. "You were able to calm his nerves in the green room, and Eric is up there talking to him like they're best friends. I can't even touch his back to guide him down a hall without his spine going board stiff. I know the reason... it just sucks."

"It's okay to have those feelings," she assures me.

I don't respond since we are in public, but I want to shout, *Is it, though?*

I'm not the one who has all of these emotional roadblocks to conquer.

I'm not the one who has PTSD from his shitty parents.

I'm not the one who is in the public eye about to make a huge announcement about his sexuality.

I shouldn't be jealous that he's letting other people calm him. No, I should be grateful he's letting me be a part of his life.

When the clip is over, the lights return to normal, and Eric beams at the camera. "Isn't that a great clip?" he asks the audience members, who cheer loudly. "While Dante is here to promote his new movie, he's also here to make a big announcement. One that you are the first to hear about," Eric informs everyone, and they applaud again. "The floor's yours, Dante."

Dante stares at Eric for a second before closing his eyes and taking a deep breath. Everything inside me is screaming to rush out and get him off the stage, to save him from having to do this, but I know I can't.

"He's going to be fine," Mel whispers, gently rubbing my back. I let out a breath I wasn't aware I was holding.

The unease rushing through my veins doesn't let up, though. I don't think it will until this is all over.

"My life has been crazy lately," Dante starts, putting on his fake smile again. "As you might have heard through the tabloids, I was drugged at a red-carpet event a while ago, and it kind of set a snowball of things into motion. I'm a private person, always have been. While I still feel like I should have the right to keep whatever I want a secret, sometimes that becomes impossible. So instead of letting people leak information about me, I'm coming out and telling you all the truth…"

He pauses, takes a deep breath, and looks at Eric, who gives him a nod of encouragement.

"I'm gay," he says softly. "I've known since I was ten, but my parents made me think it was wrong. That's why I've stayed in the closet for so long. I wasn't trying to be dishonest with anyone. I was scared. Personally, I never thought being gay was wrong, but I also didn't know how I could come out without disappointing my family. I'm done caring what they think, though, because being gay is something I want to celebrate. It's going to take me a long time to work through everything I've been through growing up, but I'm ready to do that. So, while I will still be a private person, I'm not going to hide who I am anymore. I'm Dante Michaelson, an actor and gay man."

The audience cheers, and Eric places a hand on Dante's shoulder.

"Coming out isn't easy," Eric starts after the crowd has quieted. "I remember what it was like for me. But maybe someone at home watching tonight or seeing a replay in the coming days will feel seen. They'll know they aren't the only person struggling with accepting themselves. Even millionaire actors are scared sometimes too. But there is nothing wrong with being gay. Love is love. Why should that be shamed?"

Dante nods with a big smile on his face.

"I hope so," Dante says. "I also want to announce that I will be donating one hundred thousand dollars to charities working with 2SLGBTQIA+ youth. Families should love their children no matter what, but that isn't always the case. I know by coming out today, I'll be losing my parents, so I want to support those children alienated by their families for something they have no control over."

My heart swells for this man even more.

"Wow, I'm sure that is going to make a huge difference for those children," Eric says. "Tomorrow, I'll share information on my social media for people who also want to donate and help the 2SLGBTQIA+ youth. Thank you for coming on our show and letting us be the ones you told first."

"It was easier knowing you are also a part of the community," Dante tells him, with a genuine smile this time.

"Remember to watch Dante's new movie when it comes out in theaters, and life is short, so love who you love," Eric says before a producer yells cut.

Mel, Amara, and I rush to Dante's side, but I make sure to keep my distance.

"You did amazing," Amara tells him and wraps her arms around him for a tight hug.

"I think I'm going to throw up," he whispers, and she pulls away quickly, which almost makes me laugh.

"Completely normal. You also might feel a range of things over the next little while," Mel tells him. "It's best for you to get home quickly and rest. Right now, you are on an endorphin high, and I suspect you will be crashing soon."

Even though I wish I could hug Dante, I can't, so I tilt my head. "Come on, let's go."

Amara and Mel exit in the opposite direction of us, not needing to take the back door like we do. I quickly usher Dante toward where Bennett is waiting to pick us up. Denver is instep behind us, making sure no one follows. This might seem like overkill, but none of us would feel safe without these added measures of security.

As soon as we are outside, I open the back door for Dante before tossing my keys to Denver and climbing in. Finally, I shut the door, and Bennett drives away while Denver makes his way to my car.

"I can't believe I actually did that," Dante whispers, leaning his head on my shoulder.

"You did so good, babe. I'm proud of you." My phone rings, cutting me off from saying anything else.

"What's up, Soph?" I answer after checking to see who's calling.

"We have a huge breakthrough. Come to the office."

I stare at Dante, whose eyes are barely open. I'm pretty sure he's about to fall asleep.

"Can it wait until after I get Dante to bed?"

"He's going to want to hear this," she says, and Dante smiles at me.

"Come on, this sounds good. I'll be fine," he assures me but sounds sleepy.

"You can lie down on the couch in my office," I tell him. "Bennett, change of plans... head to the office." He nods at me, making eye contact through the rearview mirror. "This better be worth it, Soph."

"It is... I promise," she says before ending the call.

Hope is always dangerous, but I feel it inside my chest. Something good is about to happen for once.

Chapter 24

Dante

NIXON GUIDES ME INTO his office, and I feel numb, my feet dragging along as my body tries to shut down from the adrenaline drop. His arm is wrapped protectively around my shoulder, offering me comfort. Normally, I'd fight this, especially since we aren't in the comfort of my house. People can see us here. But it's late, and no one is in the office except the people Nixon trusts, so I let my boyfriend hold me.

As soon as we are in Nixon's office, he gently pushes me toward a large, comfy couch, and I lie down before he turns to ruffle through his desk.

"You're crashing," he tells me, but I don't move. "Sit up, Treasure. You need to eat this." He moves me into a seated position.

I open my mouth and the taste of chocolate coats my tongue, but it's almost like I'm not fully connected with my body. After I've taken a few bites of the chocolate bar, something else is placed at my lips, and I sip the sweet orange juice.

It takes a few minutes, but it's like I finally join my body again, and my head is less foggy.

"How are you feeling?" Nixon asks, and I look into his eyes to see them filled with worry.

"Better. Sorry, I'm not sure what happened," I respond, exhaustion still weighing down on me.

"I think it was an adrenaline crash. You were so high and came down hard after making the announcement." That sounds about right. "I wanted to take you home, but Sophy has big information for us. Do you think you're ready to hear it, or should we wait a little longer?"

I take another sip of the orange juice before pushing myself to stand.

"Let's get it over with so I can go to bed. The sugar is helping the crash, but I still want to sleep this off soon." Nixon nods and stands, taking my hand to lead me to wherever Sophy is.

"Is this okay?" he asks, looking at our hands.

"It's the best," I assure him with a smile, and the way his face lights up lets me know I said the right thing.

"This better be earth-shatteringly big news," Nixon grumbles as we enter a board room where Sophy, Bennett, Denver, and a guy I don't recognize sit.

Denver has his head down, focusing intently on whatever he is working on.

"It is, I promise," she states, literally vibrating in her seat.

"Chill, babe," the guy sitting next to Sophy says.

"I'm sorry, I'm just so excited."

"I'm Slate," the guy tells me, reaching his hand forward.

"Nice to meet you." I shake his hand and sit in a chair across from them.

"Wish it was under less crazy circumstances, but Sophy is right. We found something monumental tonight."

"What is it?" I question, wondering if Nixon is as impatient for the information as I am.

"Why does everyone hate the build-up?" Sophy mumbles as she pulls up a website. "As soon as you informed me about your father's hand in everything that has been happening to you, I set up alerts for all websites he is involved in. The second anything was updated,

I would get a ping. I got two this evening *before* you made your announcement."

I finally realize what I'm staring at.

"Oh shit," I whisper as I read the words of my dad's political website.

In light of a few scandalous photos of my son, Dante Michaelson, being released, I felt it was important to make this statement after much deliberation. My wife and I are disheartened to see our son's path, but that is what happens when you leave the faith. We don't condone his behaviors or the lifestyle he is acting on, but we will continue to pray for him. Let this be a lesson for everyone out there in what happens when you abandon Jesus. Thankfully, God is merciful. Even my son can repent and change his ways. All he has to do is come back to the faith. Until then, we are cutting ties with him. We pray that maybe one day we can reconnect.

"But the photos weren't leaked... were they?" I ask, glancing at Nixon, whose brows are pulled together as he shakes his head.

Before Sophy can say anything else, a bunch of pings start ringing from her computer, and her face lights up.

"Just what I thought," she whispers, pulling up tabloid websites.

I'm stunned silent as images of Nixon and me pop up on the screen. The headlines are all some variation of *Dante Michaelson Just Broke the News He's Gay, and We've Got the Photos of the Man He's Hiding.*

"What you read was supposed to be published *after* these images were 'leaked'..." She pauses, using air quotes around the word. "Whoever is in charge of his website is an idiot and posted it *before*. It's not quite proof, but it gives us something to take to the police. It shows that they at least had information about the images before they were released. It would give them grounds to search computers and hard drives. At the very least, we should be able to nail your father with harassment. At the *most,* they might be able to charge him with attempted murder."

"Maybe the images were supposed to be released sooner, but they heard Dante's live coming out and had to rewrite the headlines," Nixon suggests.

Sophy points at him with a giant smile. "My thoughts exactly. Either way, this gives us something to run with. I've also been using my hacking software to track his whereabouts for the past few months and have found a few things he wouldn't want people finding out about..."

She pauses with what can only be described as an evil grin. We all wait for her to continue.

"Every Wednesday, your father goes to the same hotel for exactly one hour, then leaves. On those same days, a brunette sex worker shows up about fifteen minutes before he arrives and leaves ten minutes after. Coincidence? I think not."

My jaw drops as this information sinks in.

"How is my mom still with him? Does she know?" I ask, but Sophy shrugs, obviously not knowing the answer.

"One thing she *does* know about is the donations they make monthly to anti-2SLGBTQIA+ organizations. They've been made for the last ten years under your mother's maiden name."

My heart races, and I want to scream. *How could my parents do that? They are even more fucked up than I thought.*

"I've sent all the information Sophy has to my detective contact," Denver says, finally looking up from his computer.

"You mean your best friend?" Bennett adds with a lifted brow.

Denver rolls his eyes before nodding. "Yes... but contact sounds better," he grumbles as his phone rings.

"Can you meet us at the office?" Denver asks, then ends the call.

"Ford is on his way," he tells us.

I lean into Nixon a little. "I can't believe this is actually happening," I whisper to him. "Is there a chance my dad actually fucked up enough to get caught?"

"Nothing is for certain yet, but it sounds like it," he says with a smile, and my eyes start to flutter closed. My body is completely exhausted after everything that has happened in the past few days. "Come on, you can lie down in my office." Nixon pushes his chair back and offers me his hand.

"I'm glad I was here to see all of that," I tell Nixon so he doesn't feel guilty about bringing me here.

"Me too, but we still have a lot of work ahead of us. If we need you for anything, I'll come wake you up," he states as I sit on the comfortable couch.

"Can you thank everyone for working so hard on this?" I ask, finding it hard to keep my eyes open.

"You can after you've had a nap," Nixon tells me with a smirk.

This time, I don't fight to keep my eyes open. I let sleep pull me under, praying good things will happen when I wake.

Chapter 25

Nixon

WHILE I'M GLAD DANTE got to hear in real time what is happening, I still wish I had taken him home first. Everything that has happened in less than forty-eight hours is a lot, and his body is shutting down. Thankfully, the couch is comfortable to sleep on. I've done it my fair share of times, so I don't feel too bad about leaving him to rest.

"Besides releasing his statement early, do we have anything else on Dante's father?" Ford asks Sophy. She smiles so brightly in return I'm almost scared to find out what else she has up her sleeve.

"As a matter of fact, we do. We found the guy who drugged Dante."

I almost spit out the coffee I was sipping.

"Why the hell didn't you tell me?" I shout.

Sophy rolls her eyes as if I'm annoying her. "Chill, boss man, we just found him like an hour before you got here. Apparently, he's willing to talk, but we didn't want to do the interview without the police being present."

"Good call," Ford says, making a note. "Give me all the information you have on the guy. I'll bring him down for an interview at the station."

"What about Elanor? Do you think she'll talk? If she really was being blackmailed, maybe she'll be willing to throw him under the bus," Denver suggests.

"I'll bring her in for questioning as well. Arnold Michaelson has his hands in a lot of pockets. If we want him to go down for this, we have to have all our ducks in a row before we go making accusations," Ford states firmly.

"Do what you can, Ford. Dante has been through a lot, and this piece of shit is behind ninety percent of it," I supply.

"I hate guys like this, but the system is flawed. I can only do so much. I promise I'll do everything I can, though," he assures me before standing, and Denver follows, walking him out.

"You guys have done good. Thank you," I tell Sophy, Bennett, and Slate.

"It's our job to protect our clients. If we can get some good old-fashioned justice in the process... I'm all for it," Sophy says with a smirk.

"How are you holding up with everything?" Bennett asks, leaning across the table and staring at me intently.

"I'm okay," I answer, but by the way he lifts his brow, I'm not sure he believes me. Hell, I'm not sure *I* believe me, but thankfully, he doesn't push the subject.

"Dante is going to want to thank you guys in the morning, so be prepared for text messages," I state, changing the subject.

Everyone nods, and we say our goodbyes before I head to my office to wake my sleeping boy.

"Hey, handsome, it's time to go home," I whisper, stroking his cheek to wake him.

"Shh... I'm sleeping," he murmurs.

I smile. "You can sleep again when we get you to your bed."

He grumbles again but slowly stands, and instinctively, I wrap my arm around his shoulder to offer him support. He rests his head as we walk to the front desk, where Denver is waiting with my keys.

"Do you need a ride home?" I ask, but he shakes his head.

"Ford is waiting outside for me," he informs me.

"Sounds good. I'll talk to you tomorrow," I tell Denver before ushering Dante to the car.

After I buckle him in, he rests his head against the door, barely awake. By the time I get him into bed, he's once again dead to the world, and I wonder how long he's going to sleep.

"Long night, huh?" Anna asks, startling me as I reach for a glass in the dimly lit kitchen.

"You could say that." I yawn. "What are you doing up?"

"It's hard to sleep when your best friend makes a huge announcement to the world."

I nod as I fill my glass from the water dispenser on the refrigerator and sip the cold liquid.

"How is he holding up?" Anna asks.

"He's exhausted. His body kind of powered off after everything. I think tomorrow is going to be the real test to see how he's actually doing once the shock of everything wears off."

"That makes sense. Mel said he could have panic attacks this coming week that might seem out of left field, but it's normal. We'll just have to do our best to support him."

"Mel seems super nice. She looks so much like Brittany."

Anna giggles. "People ask if they are twins all the time. Mel is the older one by three years, but it's hard to believe."

I'm sure my eyes are as wide as saucers. "Yeah, I wouldn't have guessed that at all. I see why people get them mixed up for twins." Another yawn slips past my lips, and I place my hand over my mouth to cover it. "I think it's time for me to crash. I'll see you in the morning."

She says good night, and we both head to our rooms.

"You're so comfy," Dante mumbles against my chest after I've stripped and climbed into bed.

He didn't take more than two seconds to attach himself to me like the clinging sloth he is. But I love it. Holding him in my arms is perfection, and I don't want to spend another night apart.

If only things were that simple.

The next few weeks and months are going to test our relationship. I'm not certain Dante won't get scared and try to push me away. Pressuring people into doing things they don't want to do isn't something I do, so how will I convince him not to do that?

Only time will tell.

"GOOD MORNING," ANNA GRUMBLES as I flip another pancake, then pour her a cup of coffee. "You're never allowed to move out again. Breakfast and coffee I don't have to make is the way to this girl's heart," she jokes, and I chuckle.

"Really? I thought it was toe-curling kisses to the lips between your legs," Brittany teases, joining her girlfriend at the island.

Anna giggles and pecks Brittany on the lips. "That too. Obviously, penis does nothing for me, but I still want to live with Nixon forever. Or maybe when we find our own place, we can hire a personal chef," she suggests with a big toothy grin.

"Good idea. You know I suck at cooking."

I smile at the two women and how comfortable they are with each other. Dante and I are like that when it's just us and in front of Brittany and Anna, but anything else, Dante clams up. I get why, but I hope that will eventually settle.

"Dante still sleeping?" Anna questions as I hand Brittany a cup of coffee.

"Yup. When I asked him if he wanted breakfast, he responded with, 'Sleep first.' "

She nods in understanding. "Sounds like Dante. Even without a crazy hectic couple of days, he likes his beauty sleep."

"Mel said she was going to stop over this afternoon to visit. She wants to be here in case Dante needs to talk," Brittany shares.

"That's a great idea. They seem like they've gotten close."

"They really have. For the past few weeks, we've had her over regularly for movie night. I figured Dante needed more people in his life, especially after he pushed you out. Obviously, Mel isn't a replacement for you, but it's not healthy to be so secluded all the time."

"I appreciate you guys being here for him when I couldn't. I'm just happy he's letting me back in."

"Us too. You guys are perfect together," Anna voices with a cheeky grin.

I continue making breakfast, trying to stay as busy as possible so my thoughts don't drift to my time apart from Dante. Especially since there is this lingering doubt in the back of my mind saying that might happen again.

"There better be coffee," Dante murmurs as I'm plating the bacon.

"There is. Lots of food too." I fix a coffee for him the way he likes it. "How are you feeling?" I ask, placing the mug in front of him.

"Still exhausted... but I'll live."

"You did so good last night," Anna encourages in a cheery tone, but he doesn't even look at her.

"Yup... and my father still found a way to make it about what a heathen I am," he grumbles. "Have you checked the internet yet? I did before I came out here. There are literally groups being formed around how to *not* be like me."

"Why do you care what those people think?" Anna demands. "You know there isn't anything wrong with you. People are going to say shit... they always do. You can't change that. But the opinions of strangers and assholes don't matter. You know who you need to listen to? The people who actually care about you... like me, Brittany, Mel, and Nixon. Fuck everyone else."

Dante doesn't respond. His focus stays solely on something outside the kitchen window while he sips his coffee.

"Do you need anything?" I ask, setting a plate of food in front of him.

"I'm actually not hungry." He stands. "And I'd like to be alone for a little bit." With those parting words, he heads to our room, taking his cup with him.

"I thought he was doing fine with coming out," Anna whispers.

"Mel told us to expect a bunch of things. Numbness, anger, and sadness are some of them," Brittany reminds her.

"I'll check on him once I've cleaned up," I tell them before turning around, busying myself again.

"ARE YOU SURE YOU'RE not hungry?" I ask Dante as I close the bedroom door behind me.

He's sitting on the bed, staring at his phone, and I have this urge to rip it out of his hands, but I won't.

"I was so certain coming out yesterday was the right move," he whispers, not lifting his head. "But now I'm not so sure..."

"Your father was going to leak those photos no matter what," I remind him. "I'm sorry you didn't have a choice."

"I know what Anna said is right… I shouldn't care what people have to say… but I do. When you grow up being told that image is everything, something like this is a real kick in the nuts. What hurts even more is my father… my own fucking blood… was willing to tarnish my image to better his."

I make my way to the bed and sit next to Dante, wrapping my arm around his shoulder. "I'm sorry you're going through this, but you have people who actually love you and want to support you in this. I know it's easier said than done to erase everything you've been through and to let go of those lies that were fed to you, but we're here. I'm not going anywhere. If you need to fall, you can crash into my arms. I'm here to catch you, Treasure."

That's when the damn breaks, and he lets it all out, crumpling forward to cover his face with his hands. I rub his back while he sobs, not saying anything, just comforting him. Letting him know I'll always be here.

It takes a while for his tears to slow. I think it's because his body is finally releasing everything he's held onto for far too long, but I don't care how long it takes. I'll be here all day if that's what he needs.

"Eww… my hands are snotty," Dante murmurs, wiping them on his pants after he's taken a few deep breaths.

"Good thing you can wash them," I tease as he sits up and looks at me.

Swiping my thumb under his eye, I wipe away the last few stragglers of tears.

"I don't think I've ever cried like that before."

"It was well overdue, then. You know it's okay to cry, right?" I ask, and he rolls his eyes.

"Of course, I know it's okay to cry. I also know it's okay to be gay. Doesn't always make it an easy thing to accept, but I'm working on it."

"That's a good thing. We all have things we need to deal with, and it's often easier to bury those issues than to face them head-on. It makes you strong to actually be putting in the work."

"It helps having a support system too," he replies. "I'm happy you're back."

"I'm not going anywhere," I remind him, and it's a promise I intend to keep.

Dante rests his head on my shoulder, and I rub his back again, relishing having him with me again, where he belongs.

It doesn't take long before Dante's stomach grumbles, and I can't help but chuckle. "I guess someone is hungry, after all," I tease, my smile growing as he laughs.

"Feed me, lover boy," he jokes.

Nothing has ever felt more right, but we've always been good behind closed doors.

What happens when we step out of this house?

Chapter 26

Dante

Nixon's phone blares on the nightstand, pulling a low growl from my lips before I shove him and roll over. "Tell whoever it is to fuck off," I grumble. "It's too early for calls."

He chuckles and answers the call. I let out a contented sigh as the annoying ringtone shuts off, and the room becomes mostly quiet except for Nixon's low voice.

"I'll let him know," he says. "Anything else I should be aware of?" He goes quiet again, obviously listening to the caller. "Okay, thank you, please keep me updated."

"What was that about?" I ask after Nixon sets his phone down.

The moment he's back under the covers, I roll over to cuddle into his side, resting my head on his chest.

"Your father was arrested."

I gasp, propping myself up on my elbow. "Holy shit! For real?"

He nods and kisses me softly. "I doubt he'll be in jail for long, seeing who he is, but we'll make sure you can get a restraining order against him," Nixon says as I resume my cuddle position.

"I should call my lawyers," I whisper as my phone rings. "Or they'll call me." I twist and glance at the caller ID.

"Hello?" I answer, sitting up and leaning against the headboard.

Nixon does the same, wrapping his arm around my shoulder, offering me support.

"Your father was arrested," Greg informs me.

"I'm aware. Nixon just told me."

Greg chuckles. "Figures he'd get the information first. Your father's bail hearing is already scheduled for this afternoon. We will be present to demand as much as we can, but you already know the chances of him being held are extremely low."

We went over all of this when we first met about everything going on three days ago. The day after I came out.

"But you'll be able to get a restraining order, right?" I ask, even though I know it's just a piece of paper.

"Absolutely," he assures me. "There is more than enough evidence to keep him away from you. But it's highly likely the judge is going to say something along the lines of since these are the first allegations against your father and with a restraining order in place, there would be no reason to keep him in jail until we return before a jury."

"Keep me posted, please." He agrees, and I end the call. "I still can't believe they actually arrested him," I murmur, leaning my head against Nixon's shoulder.

"Guys like your father should get arrested a hell of a lot more than they do."

I couldn't agree more, but money gets people out of a lot of shit.

"Well, I'm awake now, might as well get a workout in. I want to look extra hot for the red carpet tonight," I tell Nixon, sitting up straighter and winking.

"You're still wanting to go?"

I roll my eyes without even thinking. It's the arched eyebrow and Nixon holding up one finger that alerts me to my mistake. *Well, at least I'll get an endorphin release from the spanking tonight after the event.*

"I have to live my life, Nixon. Besides, Bennett and Denver will be by my side the entire time. I'll be safe," I remind him, but his brows pull together, and his jaw ticks, clearly not happy.

"*I'll* be by your side," he corrects me, but I shake my head as I stand.

"No, *you'll* wait in the car."

"Like fuck I will."

"Don't talk to me like that."

"Why the hell don't you want me by your side?" His voice is getting louder by the second, and his face is red with anger.

Shit, I didn't think he would react like this.

"The photos of us are *everywhere*. People are going to connect the dots. You'll start getting bombarded with questions and pestering. You didn't sign up to be a celebrity. You don't need this."

He throws his hands up in frustration. "You don't get to make that decision for me."

"I'm trying to protect your personal space," I yell, my patience thinning.

"Are you really? Or do you just not want me with you?" His tone is dripping with venom, but then I realize he's reading into this more than I thought he would.

Letting out a sigh, I get on the bed again and move over to my man to kiss his cheek.

"I don't want to keep you my dirty little secret," I assure him.

"Then why haven't we announced our relationship yet?" he asks without looking at me.

We should have had this conversation sooner, but life has been hectic, to say the least.

"Because when we do, your life is going to change," I explain. "I was hoping we could give the leaked photos some time to die down first. That would also give you some time to wrap your head around everything. When we appear on a red carpet together, I want it to be as boyfriends. I want us to be prepared. I want *us* to be in control, not the interviewers and paparazzi. Tonight is already going to be a shit show, but I can handle it. It's not fair to put you through it too. I promise you'll be by my side at the next event."

His eyes stay on the ceiling as he inhales deeply, then exhales slowly and finally turns to face me.

"Really?" he asks, appearing a lot calmer now.

"Really. I should have realized that me asking you to stay back would trigger you. With how I've acted in the past, it makes sense, especially since we haven't spoken about us announcing our relationship yet. I understand you thinking I still want us to be a secret, but I don't. I'm sorry I didn't bring this up sooner."

"I'm sorry for acting like a duck," he whispers.

I stare at him like he's grown a second head. "I think you mean dick."

He smirks, shaking his head. "No, I don't. Have you ever been close to a duck? They're fucking assholes."

I can't help but laugh, and the tension between us fades.

"Are we good?" I ask after a few moments.

"We're good. Even though I'll hate every minute of it, I'll stay in the limo and only come out if something crazy happens."

I smack his chest and glare at him. "Don't say shit like that. The last red-carpet event I was at, I almost died. You're just trying to bring on bad luck by putting that out into the universe."

Nixon chuckles but pulls me into his arms, where I feel the safest.

"I'm sorry."

"Prove it," I goad him, waggling my brows.

He growls and pins me to the bed, devouring my mouth.

This man is far too good for me.

"YOU COULD PROBABLY BAIL on this event," Anna says, nibbling on her nails. I smack her hand, forcing her to stop.

"You just got your nails done. You don't want to ruin them," I chide, trying to change the subject.

"I'm nervous for you."

"I have to get out in public one day, Anna. Besides, you'll be there, along with Brittany, Nixon, Denver, Bennett, and the other body-guards. I'll be safe."

"It's not your physical well-being I'm worried about."

This is the first red carpet I will be walking alone. She knows how much that terrifies me. Anna has always kept my anxiety at bay. Without her by my side each step of the way, I'm not sure how I'm going to handle it. She's also worried about everyone bombarding me with questions about *everything* going on in my life But honestly, my queerness is the least of my fears tonight. Having a panic attack in the middle of a red carpet is the biggest one.

Part of me wants to change my mind and ask Nixon to walk with me. But I meant what I told him earlier—he needs time. I refuse to throw him to the wolves.

"Hey, handsome, are you ready to walk the red carpet?" Mel asks, startling me as she walks out with Brittany.

"What are you doing here?" I question, taking in how elegant she looks.

"Figured you might want a friend by your side tonight. You told me how Anna has always been your rock, so I'm here." She twirls in her gorgeous emerald-green dress, and I chuckle and pull her in for a hug.

"Thank you," I whisper into her neck.

"Ready to go?" Nixon asks after he gets off a call and kisses my cheek.

I beam at him and nod. "Come on, ladies, let's go rock that red carpet," I call out, and we make our way to the limo.

THE EVENT GOES BY smoothly, with Amara making it clear any questions about my sexuality or father will be ignored, and we will move on. So thankfully, I get to talk about my work and upcoming projects while Mel keeps my anxiety under control.

It was a pretty amazing night, but I won't lie and say I didn't wish Nixon was by my side. It would have been a fantastic night had it not been for the worry in the pit of my stomach.

When the event is over, we climb into the limo, and I hug Nixon.

"How did it go?" he asks, then gently presses his lips to mine.

"Better than I thought it would, but Amara was a boss bitch. I missed you, though."

He smiles and nods. "Me too. Why don't we get together with Amara in the next couple of days to make a plan to announce our relationship officially? That way, I won't have to stay back again."

I beam at him and lean in for another kiss. "I love that idea."

I lean into Nixon's side as we make our way home, everyone falling into easy conversations. I love how comfortable this feels right now. Yet it also dawns on me we've only been able to have moments like this with my friends so far. Now that I'm out, that doesn't seem fair to Nixon anymore.

As we drive, an idea pops into my head. Now to put it into motion.

"WHAT ARE YOU DOING here?" Nixon asks as his friends and employees walk through our front door.

"Didn't you get the memo? It's game night," Denver teases with a soft shove.

Nixon looks at me, and I shrug. "I figured it would be nice to hang out with your friends too, so I got Denver to send out the invites."

"Second time you've kept a secret from me." Nixon growls at Denver, who bristles before Nixon slaps him on the shoulder. "But it's fine. I get why you did it."

"Anyone want to help me with this food?" a guy I don't recognize shouts, coming inside with platters of food.

"On it," Bennett replies, racing outside to help.

"You can put that in the kitchen," I tell him.

He nods in thanks. "I'm Ford, by the way. It's nice to meet you."

"Likewise," I say with a tight smile as more people I don't recognize enter the house. "I told you to only invite those close to Nixon," I whisper to Denver, my tone letting him know I'm not joking around.

"I did," he assures me. "Ford is my friend and is crashing at my house right now since his girlfriend kicked him out. The good-looking dude and the pretty brunette are old clients of Nixon's that he grew close to. Other than that, it's just the crew from work. Is that too much?" He now looks unsure of himself.

I take a deep breath and shake my head. "It's fine. Sorry, I guess seeing everyone is just triggering my anxiety. Don't let Nixon know I'm freaking out a little."

Denver chuckles. "That's an easy secret to keep. But I promise, they're all good people. You can let your guard down. Besides, if anyone tried anything, Nixon would kick the shit out of them."

I laugh as I search for the man who has stolen my heart. He's standing by the door, casually talking with the gorgeous couple, so I make my way over to them.

"Hi, I'm Dante," I say, reaching my hand out to them.

"I'm Dax, and this is my wife, Izzy," the man says, shaking my hand. It takes a moment, but the names finally connect.

"You're the doctor who helped out Nixon not too long ago."

"That's me. I'm glad I was able to help. Also, sorry you had to deal with that."

"It's been a lot, but hopefully, life stops being so hectic for us," I reply.

"I get that. Nixon was my bodyguard when shit was hitting the fan for me," Izzy informs me. "I'm glad he found someone to make him happy, especially since he wouldn't let me set him up with my brother."

Nixon laughs. "He wasn't my type."

"And what exactly is your type?" I ask him with a smirk.

"A gorgeous brat," he grumbles, bending down to give me a gentle kiss.

I feel like I should be freaking out right now, but I'm not. Maybe it's because I'm in the safety of my home, and if Nixon trusts these people, then I do too.

"I brought *Monopoly*," Sophy yells.

Nixon groans. "That girl is the *worst* when it comes to board games. If she wins, she's gloating. If she loses, she's the biggest spoiled sport there is," he whispers.

"Thanks for letting me know," I say before shouting, "Nixon and I are in."

That earns me a swat on the ass and a growl in my ear. "You've missed your spankings, haven't you?"

My body shivers with anticipation, and I shrug and wink at him. "I feel like you're just making empty promises right now," I tease and rush over to Sophy and Slate.

"TODAY WAS AMAZING," NIXON says after our guests have left.

"I'll admit, I was nervous, but I had a great time. Your friends are amazing. I can't wait to meet your parents next."

Nixon steps forward and grips my hips with his strong hands, sending a shiver down my spine as he pulls me into him and crashes his lips to mine. "You make me so fucking happy," he whispers against my lips once we break for air.

"I love you, Nixon. I hope you see I'm trying. It isn't always going to be easy for me, especially in public, but I want to be the man you deserve."

Nixon whispers kisses against my lips, and I smile. "Babe, if you're never comfortable with public displays of affection, I'll live with that. But it means the world to me that you're willing to let my friends in. My parents will also love you as much as I do."

I kiss him sweetly before grabbing his hand and giving it a little tug. "I was promised a spanking," I remind him with a smirk, then drop his hand and bolt for the bedroom.

"Your ass is mine, Brat."

I laugh as his loud footsteps follow me down the hall. I barely have time to turn around once I've reached the room before Nixon grabs me and throws me on the bed.

"Get naked, *now*," Nixon growls out with a look of pure lust that makes my heart race.

Obeying as fast as I can, I shuck my clothes and lie naked on the bed, waiting for what my man has up his sleeve.

"Get over my knees, Brat," Nixon commands.

Again, I listen without complaint. It's been far too long since Nixon spanked me, and I've missed our impact play sessions more than I thought possible.

"I've missed turning this perfect ass the shade of a tomato." Nixon rubs my ass firmly. "How many spankings do you think you need tonight?"

I turn my face a bit so I can look at him. "You decide. I trust you."

"I was thinking ten."

I nod, knowing it's going to hurt but also certain Nixon will be there to take care of me afterward. We both need this for too many reasons to list.

A loud smack fills the room, followed by the delicious sting of the spank. I smile and count. "One."

The spanks come hard and fast, and he alternates between cheeks, leaving me a puddle of goo when he's finished.

"You did so fucking good," Nixon praises, pulling me into his arms and holding me for a moment. Then he lays me on the bed and leaves to get supplies.

"Will you fuck me?" I ask as soon as he's in the room again. "I'm so hard it hurts, and I want you to punish my ass in more ways than one."

Nixon grins and opens the drawer for the lube, but I stop him as he reaches for a condom.

"Can we go bare tonight?"

Nixon eyes me warily, and I wonder if this is too soon.

"I haven't been with anyone in years and was negative for everything the last time I was tested," I tell him, trying to ease some of his worries. "I trust you. If you're comfortable, I want this with you."

"I've never been bare with a partner before," he admits, and I'm happy I'll hopefully get to be his first.

"I love you, Nixon, but if you're not ready for this, I understand."

"I'm ready, Treasure. It just feels so surreal. I thought I had lost you when you pushed me away. I don't ever want to feel like that again. It's early, but you're it for me. I don't ever want anyone else. So, if you're positive you're all in, then I'm ready."

A mixture of pride and hurt fills my chest, and I reach for his hand. "I'm sorry I hurt you, but I feel the same way. I'm all in, baby. I don't want anyone else."

Nixon eagerly gets on the bed, kissing me with all the love inside him. My heart races as his tongue dips into my mouth, battling with mine. Words are great, but actions like this prove he isn't only telling me what I want to hear. No, it's so evident in the way he steals my breath that he is just as crazy about me as I am about him.

"Need you," I plead after we break apart, panting for air.

"I've got you." He picks up the bottle of lube and pours a generous amount onto his fingers.

I pull my knees up to give him better access and am met with a cold finger pressed against my puckered entrance.

"Your ass is fucking perfect," Nixon mutters, his finger breaching the hole.

My eyes roll into the back of my head. "Yesss," I hiss out as he wiggles the digit around before adding in a second.

He works me while pressing kisses to my inner thighs and stomach, whispering words of praise and adoration. When he moves his fingers just right, hitting the spot of pleasure inside me, I cry out, and my cock bobs hard against my skin.

Shit, am I going to come untouched tonight? That would be a first.

"Are you ready, Treasure?" Nixon asks after a third finger has worked me good.

"Please. I need you," I beg, and Nixon smirks.

Another dollop of lube is spread onto Nixon's giant cock before he grabs my ankles and places them on his shoulder. Then he lines himself up and gently sinks in.

"Fuck I've missed you so much." I moan as he pushes all the way in.

"Our bodies were made for each other," he notes as he leans down to kiss me. "I love you so fucking much, Dante."

"And I love you," I whisper, tears coming to my eyes at the intimacy of this moment. "Now fuck me like you mean it," I encourage Nixon, bringing a grin to his gorgeous face.

"With pleasure, Treasure."

He finally lets loose, and I scream, "Fuck" as he pounds into me before adjusting my hips so he's nailing my prostate.

Each thrust pushes me closer to the edge, and I swear I'm seeing stars from how amazing this feels. Nixon doesn't let up his punishing pace, and a few moments later, I'm coming, untouched. My entire body spasms, and I've never felt anything so intense in my entire life. My cock leaks as he milks my prostate, but this isn't a normal orgasm.

"Holy shit, you look hot right now," Nixon tells me, fucking me like a madman and stroking my still-hard cock.

As he pounds into me, another sensation takes over my body, and I erupt like a fucking fountain, covering my abs and chest with cum, a few drops landing on my face from the force. That's all it takes for my sexy man to reach his own climax, shooting his cum deep into my channel.

Nixon holds me, his softening cock still inside me, and I've never felt anything so special.

"Why don't we have a shower? Then I'll apply some cream to your ass before we cuddle, and you can have some chocolate," Nixon suggests.

"That sounds amazing," I tell him as he gently pulls out, leaving me feeling empty. But the sensation of his cum leaking out of me reminds me of what we just did—how special this moment is.

Nixon takes my hand, leading me to the bathroom without saying a word. He turns on the shower, ensuring the temperature is right before guiding me in. I rest my head on his chest as the water cascades over us, and I realize how perfect this feels. I might have been forced out of the closet, but at least I got a perfect man in exchange.

I only pray my past doesn't continue to haunt us.

Chapter 27

Nixon

Today, Dante and I are shopping for supplies for the Brazil trip, which is fast approaching.

I still can't believe it's been three weeks since Dante came out, and we are leaving in a week for six months.

Our relationship has been progressing amazingly, and for the most part, the paparazzi are leaving us alone. Thankfully, it doesn't take them long to latch onto the next story.

"I think you'd look hot in this," Dante tells me, holding up the ugliest T-shirt I've ever seen.

I lift a brow at him as if to say, "Really?" which makes him laugh so hard people turn to stare. "I think I have enough clothes," I mutter.

Dante rolls his eyes, bringing a smirk to my lips as I hold up three fingers to remind him how many spankings he's already on. His cheeks turn a gorgeous shade of pink, but he doesn't respond.

"All of your clothes are black. I'm not sure how you don't die in that attire. Why not pick something fun?"

"My job is to blend into the background. Black makes that easy."

He sticks his tongue out at me. "You're no fun. Besides, you aren't *just* a bodyguard anymore. You're my boyfriend, and I want you to have fun clothes."

The pout he gives me is almost too much to argue with. "You can pick out three solid color shirts, but that's it," I concede, and Dante dances around with joy.

When we're done shopping, we head to the car, which is parked a couple of blocks away since the streets were packed when we got here.

"Dante," a female calls out, and instinctively, I move closer to him.

Dante turns, his face going pale as he drops his bag.

"Babe, are you okay?" I ask quietly.

He stays frozen, staring at the woman. That's when I realize who she is.

This woman looks exactly like every photograph I've seen her in. Completely put together with a well-practiced smile that doesn't reach her eyes, which are the same color as her son's. I know the evil behind that fake and high-priced exterior, and it's downright ugly.

"You shouldn't be here, Mrs. Michaelson," I advise her.

"Why not? It's a free country," she bites out. "Besides, the little shit beside you ruined my life." She glares at Dante.

"How the hell did I do that?"

"Your father is going to end up in prison because of you. Don't think I don't know it was you and your boyfriend who leaked the information about him hiring escorts." She sneers. "I'm the laughing fucking stock of this town now, and it's all because of you." She raises her hand to strike him, but I'm quicker and grab her wrist.

"Don't you dare touch him," I growl out.

"Why should I listen to the man who defiled my son?"

"Get fucked, Mom," Dante spits out.

His mother gasps and stumbles back. "The devil really does have a hold of you. You're both going to burn in hell," she shouts over her shoulder as she turns and rushes away.

"Holy shit," Dante mutters, shaking his head.

"Your mom seems like a real peach," I supply, bringing a small smile to my handsome boyfriend's lips.

"Think we can get a restraining order against her too?"

"It's worth reaching out to your lawyers about," I offer. "Has she ever been physical with you before?"

Dante shakes his head. "Honestly, she was just more indifferent to me. Wasn't as obvious about her hatred like my father… not until now, anyway. At least she showed her real colors today. That way, I won't feel bad about cutting ties with her too. I'm happy they aren't in my life anymore. I'm better off without them."

I nod, pulling him into my arms for a hug. He stiffens, and it's then I remember we're in public.

"I'm sorry," I whisper as I let him go.

"I'm the one who's sorry. I promise I'm working on getting better at public displays of affection, but it's going to take some time."

"Take all the time you need. I'm not going anywhere."

He smiles, but I can tell he's still shaken up about everything that went down.

"Come on, let's go home." I tilt my head toward the crosswalk.

We walk to the car. Dante is a few steps ahead, even though I wish I could hold his hand. Unfortunately, he's not ready for that yet. So I'll have to be patient.

The light turns green as Dante reaches the street, but the second his feet hit the asphalt, a car steps on the gas, nailing him hard. He flies over the roof, and the car speeds off, leaving his limp body on the street.

"No," I yell so loud my throat hurts as I rush to him.

Acting on instinct, I pull my phone out and dial 9-1-1, replaying what happened.

"Don't leave me, Treasure," I whisper as his eyes remain closed.

I just got the love of my life back, and now I might be losing him a second time. This one permanent.

"WHERE IS HE?" ANNA asks, rushing into the hospital.

"Surgery," I reply, staring at the cup of coffee I'm holding.

I haven't taken a single sip, but a nurse was nice enough to bring it to me, so I feel bad about getting rid of it.

"Do we know anything?" She sits beside me.

I shake my head. "He didn't look good, Anna, and they won't tell me anything else. You're listed as his power of attorney, so you'll be able to get the information."

"He's strong. He won't die," Anna assures me, but I doubt she fully believes those words.

It's just something people say, but life is a finicky bitch, and it doesn't matter how strong Dante is. If it's his time to go, nothing can keep him here. I pray to whatever deity is listening that it isn't his time.

"MISS APPLEYARD," A NURSE calls out, and Anna and I stand quickly.

"This is Dante's boyfriend," Anna supplies when the nurse gives me a funny look.

"The doctor wants to talk with you," the nurse tells us, and we follow her to a small room.

The walls are a weird shade of pink, and it has that overly clean hospital smell. A couch and two large chairs line the walls, and a light wood coffee table sits in the middle.

"This looks like a room where they tell people their loved one has died," I whisper.

Anna nods. Tears are brimming in her eyes, so I pull her into my arms. That's when she lets go. *Fuck, I hope our thoughts aren't true, but even if they are, I can't break down yet.*

"I'm Dr. Fontain," an elderly man in a white lab coat greets us a few minutes later.

"Nice to meet you. Can you please tell us about Dante?" Anna begs.

"Mr. Michaelson received multiple injuries, including internal bleeding that required immediate surgery, but we were able to stabilize him."

"He isn't dead?" Anna whispers.

The doctor shakes his head. "He isn't out of the woods yet, and he's resting, but as of right now, he's stable. There is a long road to recovery ahead of him, and the next few days are vital to how this turns out."

Anna flings herself into my arms, sobbing tears of relief.

"When can we see him?" I ask.

"You're welcome to go in now. We still have Dante under a light sedative to make sure his body has ample time to heal. He'll be asleep, but we always recommend talking to the patients. We can't know for sure if he hears you, but positive words never hurt," he tells us before standing and leading us to the room.

I fight back a gasp when my eyes land on Dante. The lower half of his body is almost entirely in a cast. Only one leg isn't restrained.

Anna asks the question that's floating around in my head. "Is he going to be able to walk again?"

"He broke his pelvis and one leg in multiple places, but he is young and healthy, so he has a good chance at making a full recovery. Like I said, as soon as we get past these few days of observation, we'll know more," he states, then leaves us alone with Dante.

Pulling a chair over to the side of the bed with the least number of obstacles, I reach for his hand and gently squeeze it.

"I'm here, Treasure," I assure him. "You heal so you can come back to me."

"Do you want to go home and get changed?" Anna asks, resting her hand on my shoulder.

"I don't want to leave him," I reply, not taking my eyes off Dante. "I *can't* leave him. I already failed him once."

It's like my body can't fight the emotions anymore, and tears cascade down my face.

"You didn't fail him," Anna assures me, but I shake my head as sobs rack my body.

"I did, Anna. It was my job to keep him safe, and I failed."

She rubs my back while I let it all out. I am glad she's here with me. I'm not sure I'd be able to do this on my own.

"I'm sorry," I whisper, wiping my face once my tears have slowed.

"You have nothing to be sorry about. I understand why you're beating yourself up, but there is no way you could have known that vehicle was going to gun it. No one could have pulled him back fast enough unless they were a superhero," she tells me, but it's still hard to believe.

I don't say anything else. I simply keep my eyes on my boy. "I love you, Dante," I whisper as I rub my thumb over the top of his hand.

I hope the universe is done playing games with my heart and brings Dante out of this alive. I also pray he forgives me for letting this happen.

Chapter 28

Dante

Buzzing, beeping, and the soft sound of snoring fills my ears as I try to open my eyes, but they feel like they weigh a hundred pounds.

A little whimper leaves my lips as I force my eyes to open. That's when a warm hand squeezes mine. "Dante?" I hear the voice I love that belongs to the person who means the world to me whisper, and I want to see his face so badly.

Why won't my eyes open?

"Take your time, Treasure," he tells me, rubbing his thumb on my hand.

A ringing noise fills the room.

Where the hell are we?

I take deep breaths and put all my focus on opening my eyes. Then, finally, they flutter open, and I'm face to face with the love of my life. "Hi," I whisper, but my throat feels hoarse.

"Careful, you've been asleep for a few days, and they had a tube down your throat during surgery."

"Our actor is finally awake?" a female with a sweet voice asks.

"I heard him whimpering," Nixon tells the lady.

"Do you know where you are, Mr. Michaelson?" the lady asks me, and when I look at her, it dawns on me.

"Hospital?"

She smiles, her face warm and kind. "You are correct. Your doctor is on his way, but do you need anything until he gets here?"

"Water," I say quietly, my throat itchy and burning.

"Absolutely. I'll be right back with a cup and a straw."

The moment she's gone, Nixon kisses my forehead.

"I'm so happy you're back," he tells me with glassy eyes.

"I'm sorry I scared you," I whisper as the nurse places the cup on a table and rolls it over to the bed.

"I'm going to check your vitals real quick," she says. "Are you in any pain?"

"A little," I reply, then Nixon holds the cup to my mouth, and I slowly sip the water. "More just achy all over."

"That's normal. I'm going to give you a little extra pain reliever in your IV. I'll let your doctor explain the recovery plan to you when he gets here, but in the meantime, let me know if anything really starts to hurt."

I nod at her and turn my attention back to Nixon.

"What the hell happened?" I ask him since my memory is foggy.

"You were hit by a car. It was actually your mother driving."

I gasp, and he squeezes my hand.

"We found out the day after. The police arrested her. She isn't even being let out on bail since it was attempted homicide."

"I can't believe she would do that." I shake my head.

"She's pleading temporary insanity. Claims she was just so angry she blacked out and has no recollection of hitting you. I doubt it will hold up in court, though."

"Both my parents could be in prison soon. This is fucking insane."

"Good evening, Mr. Michaelson," an older man with white hair greets me. "I'm happy to see you awake. I'm Dr. Fontain. How are you feeling?"

"Like I got hit by a car," I respond dryly, making the doctor snicker.

"So you remember what happened?"

I shrug. "It's foggy, but bits and pieces seem to be coming back. Nixon filled me in, though."

"Foggy memory is completely normal," he assures me. "When the car hit you, your left leg and pelvis broke on impact. There was also some internal bleeding that we tended to during surgery. You've been asleep for a few days while your body healed, and we monitored your progress. You still have a long road of recovery ahead of you, but the prognosis is promising. You'll just have to put in the hard work and listen to your team."

"I'll do my best."

"That's all we ask. It looks like you have an amazing support system here, which is also important when it comes to healing."

"When do I get to go home?" I ask, wanting to get out of the hospital as soon as possible.

I've never been a big fan of doctors in general, and being around sick people gives me the ick. But at least they were able to save my life.

"Now that you're awake, we want to monitor you for a little bit longer, but you should be able to be released in a few days. Normally, we would send patients to a physical rehabilitation center, but you would have the option to go home as long as you have the correct staff to take care of you."

"I'll arrange for that," Nixon assures him and puts a note into his phone.

"Do you have any other questions?" the doctor asks me, and I shake my head. "If you do, feel free to ask a nurse. In the meantime, make sure you get lots of rest, don't fight your body to stay awake. I'll be back to check on you tomorrow."

As soon as he leaves, I turn my attention to my sexy bodyguard.

"Thank you for being here," I tell Nixon, and he gently lifts my hand and places a soft kiss on my knuckles.

"I wouldn't be anywhere else."

My eyes become heavy again, and Nixon gingerly kisses my forehead.

"Sleep, Treasure. I'll be here when you wake."

I don't have the strength to fight the sleep, so I listen, letting it pull me under.

"You look like shit," Anna tells me, walking into the room with a cheeky grin.

Nixon only left a few minutes ago to get something to eat. He knew Anna was on her way, and I wanted a moment alone before she showed up. I love that man, but when you're stuck in a hospital bed, there aren't many moments to be alone and breathe. I needed some space, even if it was only for a second.

"I think that happens when you get hit by a car" I reply, pulling the corners of my lips up.

"I'm so glad you're alive," she whimpers, rushing over to me.

I'm sure she's about to crash into me when she stops suddenly. Her eyes comb over my body, and she's figuring out how best to hug me without hurting me. After a moment, she slowly leans in to kiss my cheek and holds me gently.

We stay like that for a bit, neither of us saying anything.

"You are not allowed to leave me," she whispers after. When she pulls away, tears are in her eyes, and she sits on the edge of my bed, holding my hand.

"It's not like I planned for my mother to hit me with her car," I joke, hoping to get a smile, but a few tears break free and trail down her cheek.

"I was so scared."

"I'm sorry," I respond, hating that she and Nixon had to endure that. "I keep thinking that if I were holding Nixon's hand, this wouldn't have happened because he'd have yanked me out of there," I admit. "If I didn't have all this anxiety around public displays of affection, I could have avoided hurting you."

Anna's eyes go wide. "Don't you dare try to take the blame for this. The only one guilty here is your mother. May she rot in jail."

I smirk at her words. "Still, I need to keep up my therapy. Nixon deserves a stronger partner."

"You *are* strong, sweetie," she assures me. "Not many people have gone through all the shit you have. You're putting in the work to get through this already, so don't beat yourself up, okay?"

"Okay."

"Let's just focus on getting you out of here," she states, changing the subject, and I'm thankful for it.

"How are you feeling?" Amara questions as she walks into my room.

I've been in here for almost a week now, and I get to go home tomorrow. To say the least, I'm beyond excited.

Amara and I have been talking a lot on the phone, but this is her first time visiting. She wanted to give me a bit of space for a few days.

"I'm all right. How is everything going on your end? Are the producers pissed I have to push back filming?"

"Obviously, people are upset, but your lawyers made fantastic contracts, and they can't fire you over this. I only want your focus to be on healing. I'll deal with everything else. Everyone is well aware you will not be back to work for at least six months."

"Thank you."

"That's what you pay me for," she jokes. "Did you get Dante's occupational therapist and nurse to sign the NDA agreements?" she asks Nixon, who is sitting in the corner of the room, working on his computer.

"Yup. I emailed them to you this morning," Nixon informs her.

"Are you excited to go home tomorrow?" she asks me.

"More than I could ever express. Hospitals suck."

"I didn't realize we were that bad," Caitlyn, one of the nurses who has been working with me since I got here, teases.

I laugh. "You're the only good thing about this place."

She giggles, waving her hand at me. "I understand wanting to go home. No one wants to stay in a hospital longer than necessary."

She takes my vitals, and I turn my attention back to Amara. "How is everything going on the social media front?"

"Really good. I hate that your mom ran you over, but it's turned the conversation about you on its head. It's got people talking and moving the topic onto a wider range of things instead of focusing solely on your coming out. Your fans seem to really be on your side, and people are wishing you a speedy recovery. Even those who originally were upset about your announcement have started to show support for you, admitting that they were wrong and love is love. For now, I think it will stay as is until your parents' trials."

"Makes sense. Do we have a date for those yet?"

"Not officially. Your father's will be first. They are saying it's anywhere from twelve to eighteen months away. Your parents' lawyers, however, are requesting to set up a meeting with you and your lawyers in a few weeks when you feel up to it." I sigh.

"They are going to try talking you into helping them get lesser charges," Nixon adds.

"Can I ignore them?"

"Why don't we have your lawyers over next week?" Nixon suggests. "You can see what they think about this meeting."

I nod, wondering if going through with this shit show is even going to be worth it. Maybe I should take the settlement. But if I do that, my father wins, and I *can't* let him win. He is the reason I'm so fucked in the head. And my mother is the reason I'm lying in this hospital bed. My parents need to pay for what they did.

I'm done taking the easy way out. I have amazing people in my corner now. Even if taking my parents down drains me completely, I know my real family will be there to pick me up when it's all over.

"How are you feeling?" Mel asks.

I roll my eyes. "Getting really sick of that question," I mutter.

It's been a week since I've been home, and this is my first therapy session since the accident.

"I bet, but you know we mean well."

I sigh but nod. "I know. I just want to be healed physically and mentally so I can move on with my life already."

"Well, let's work on that mental health," she says.

I inhale slowly, holding it for a moment before blowing it out. I know I'm going to be exhausted after this, but it will be worth it in the long run.

I have four to six months of healing and physical therapy before I'll return to normal, or so the doctors say. I'm going to put in the same amount of effort to get my mental health on the right track too.

Chapter 29

Nixon

Six Months Later

Izzy wraps her slim arms around Dante's neck with a giant smile. I can't help but grin at the motion.

"You did amazing today," she shouts, only slightly out of breath.

"You really did, babe. I'm so proud of you," I tell him.

As soon as Izzy lets him go, I pull him close and give him a quick kiss, not caring that we are sweaty.

"I can't believe we ran that long, and I still feel great," he says, beaming. He lifts his shirt to wipe the sweat off his brow.

Of course, I let my eyes roam over his abs of steel.

"I think you're officially done with physical therapy," Izzy states.

"Does that mean I can finally get fucked?" he asks as she takes a sip of water, making her spray it everywhere as she laughs.

I can't help but shake my head with a smirk.

"I know you've been cleared for mild sexual activities for a while, but yeah, I think you can get back to whatever you enjoy now. Just remember to listen to your body. If things hurt, don't do it," Izzy reminds him in a firm tone.

"I know. Thank you so much for your help. I wouldn't be where I am today without your help. You're a kickass occupational therapist," he tells her, and her cheeks turn a bright shade of pink.

"You were a pretty good patient for an adult," she jokes.

Izzy graduated this year, and while her goal is to mainly work with pediatric patients as an occupational therapist, she agreed to take Dante on before starting work as an independent contractor. Both Dante and I trust her, so we were happy she was willing to work with him for his recovery.

"Are you and Dax coming over for the barbeque this weekend?" he asks.

Izzy beams at him. After knowing her during the worst time of her life, I couldn't be happier that she has so much life in her again. "Of course. We wouldn't miss your last get-together before you and Nixon leave us for half a year."

"We'll miss you all, but I'm happy to finally be going back to work. It's been too long, and I miss acting."

I'm a bit nervous about being gone for so long, but I would never let Dante go to Brazil for six months without me.

We'll be back a few weeks before his father's court date. As much as we're both dreading it, it will be nice for it to be over. His mother, on the other hand, took a deal and won't be going to court. She'll still spend a good amount of time in jail, but we won't have to sit through a second trial. Thank fuck.

Brazil will be good to keep our minds off of everything.

Thankfully, a lot of my job can be done remotely, and Denver is taking over any in-person appointments I normally would have done. In a way, this is a great start to move me into a more behind-the-scenes position, which has been necessary for a long time but something I was fighting.

My love has always been my job, and that was being a bodyguard. I didn't want to push papers all day. But I have a new love now—Dante. Work isn't my only purpose in life anymore. We've even been talking about the possibility of growing our family in the near future. The idea makes me happier than I ever dreamed possible.

"I'll see you both in two days," Izzy shouts as she heads to her car.

We wave as she drives away and then go into the house.

"Did you hear what the lady said?" Dante asks, waggling his brows.

"I did, but I'm not sure if you've been a good enough boy to earn something like that."

He gasps. "I've been the *best* boy!"

I step closer to him, leaning down to silence him with a kiss. "You're right. You've been amazing. But as much as I want to fuck you, we have dinner with my parents in a few hours, so that will have to wait."

Dante rolls his eyes, and I click my tongue at him. "Cleared to get fucked and already looking to get a good spanking too, I see." He snickers. "Get your ass in the shower now, and maybe I'll let you come before dinner," I command, laughing while Dante runs as fast as his legs will carry him.

I'm so happy about how far Dante has come since his accident. It wasn't an overnight thing. It's taken six fucking months of hard work, but he's back to the man he was when I first met him. Actually, that's wrong. He's a stronger man now, both physically and mentally. He's pushed himself as hard as he could to heal as much as possible, and I couldn't be prouder of him.

I've also spent my fair share of time speaking with a therapist of my own. After seeing Dante get hit by that car, I knew I had things I needed to work through with a professional, and I'm glad I did.

The accident turned our lives upside down again, but we came out the other side stronger than ever.

"It's so nice to see you again," Mom gushes, pulling Dante into her arms.

"At least I look better this time," Dante jokes.

Mom and Dad came down shortly after Dante's accident to show him their support. It was a great visit, but I know this one will be even better.

"It is good to see you walking," she replies with a genuine smile. "I still can't believe my boys are leaving for Brazil for six months."

Mom told Dante the last time she was down that she was now his mother since his was so rotten.

"It will go by faster than you think," he promises as the hostess comes to take us to our table.

"I'm sure it will, but I'm still going to worry. It's what good mothers do," she tells him as we take our seats at the back of the restaurant.

"It's what good *parents* do," my dad corrects her with a cheeky grin, looking at both Dante and me. "We love you both, and we're not sorry for being worry warts."

"We promise to call often," Dante assures them. "It's nice having people who care about me." He adds the last part quietly.

I reach over to squeeze his hand, and he beams at me. That's something else that has taken time and patience, but he's no longer afraid of physical touch in public.

Dante loves to grab my hand when we're walking down the street or steal a quick kiss here and there because he *just had to*. At least, that's what he tells me. I love that he's strong enough to do that now.

"We'll always be in your corner," Mom says with kind eyes, and he reaches across the table to grab her hand.

"Thank you."

After dinner, we say goodbye to my parents, who are staying at a hotel even though Dante insisted they stay with us. It's not like we don't have the room. But my parents wanted to give us space, and I appreciate that. It didn't stop Dante from putting his credit card on file at the hotel they are staying at. I'm sure they'll give him hell for that later.

"Ready to get home?" I ask my handsome boyfriend as we walk toward my SUV, hand in hand.

"Yes, Sir," he purrs, and it goes straight to my dick.

"Since you've been a good boy, I've decided I'm going to fuck you so hard you forget your name tonight," I whisper into his ear as we pause at the lights before crossing the street to where the car is parked.

His body vibrates next to mine, and his pupils dilate as he stares at me with lust written all over his face.

"I can't wait." He licks his lips.

Again, my cock strains against the confines of my boxers. I need to get Dante home *now*.

On the drive, our sexual tension is heavy. I wrap my hands tightly around the steering wheel, preventing me from reaching over and resting my hand on Dante's knee, which bounces with pent-up sexual frustration. Thankfully, he keeps his hands firmly in his lap and his focus out the window. Things will be explosive as soon as we touch each other, and my concentration needs to be on the road.

Everything is a blur after we pull into the driveway as we waste no time heading straight for the bedroom.

"Over my knees," I command the moment we are both naked, and I'm sitting on the edge of the bed.

Dante doesn't fight me, doing exactly as he's told.

"Such a good boy," I praise, rubbing my hand gently over his bubble butt. "I'm going to give you four quick spankings, then I'm going to fuck you hard and fast. Are you ready?"

"More than ready."

I lick my lips as I caress his skin before lifting my hand and bringing it down hard on his right ass cheek. The smack fills the room, and Dante cries out before counting like the perfect sub he is.

With each spank, his creamy skin turns a brighter shade of red, and I'm sure his ass stings as much as my palm does. By the time he screams four, my cock is throbbing, and his is leaking precum against my thigh.

"You did so good, Treasure," I tell him, moving him to kneel beside me on all fours. "I can't wait to be buried balls deep inside you."

We've been intimate since the accident, but this is the first time I'm going to be inside him since then. I'm sure his body was ready sooner, but I wasn't. I needed to make sure he was healed completely. But after his run today, I'm certain he'll be okay. However, that won't stop me from keeping the closest eye on him the entire time I fuck him. One wrong look, and I'll stop. I refuse to hurt the man I love.

The moment Dante is in position, I kneel behind him and pull his cheeks apart, my mouth watering with need.

"Your body is perfection."

"Gah" is his response as I lap at his hole.

"So fucking good." I groan before going back for another taste.

I take my time, fucking him with my tongue before I move to the nightstand to grab the bottle of lube from the drawer. As much as I love eating his ass, I know I need to stretch him well.

After my fingers are coated, I slowly slide in one, watching Dante's reaction closely.

"Shit..." he hisses out, his mouth hanging open with a look of pure ecstasy taking over his face.

Thankfully, his body doesn't resist me too much, and it doesn't take long before I'm fucking him with my finger.

"How's that feeling, Treasure?" I ask as I slide in and out of him gently.

"So good. Want more, please," Dante begs.

Carefully, I move in a second finger, waiting until his body relaxes so I can shove it all the way in.

"Yes," Dante cries out as I find the hardness of his prostate and rub it.

"I love how loud you are," I tell him, scissoring my fingers to prepare him for my cock.

After a few minutes of two fingers, I shove in a third, then a fourth. By the time I'm sure he's ready for me, my cock is so hard it's fucking painful, and Dante is a panting mess.

"On your back, Treasure," I instruct, pulling my fingers from his delectable ass.

He obeys eagerly, and I slick my cock with a good coating of lube.

"I love you," I remind him as I pull him to the edge of the bed and line up.

We groan as I leisurely slide inside him, his legs wrapping around my waist and my eyes rolling to the back of my head. "Fuck." I grunt as his body grips me tightly. I'm not sure how I'm going to last.

"You feel so good inside me," Dante murmurs.

Leaning down, I seal my lips over his, needing a moment before I can start moving. I don't need to be a two-pump chump here, and I swear he's tighter than the first time we had sex.

"This is exactly where I'm meant to be," I whisper against Dante's lips.

"I love you," he replies and kisses me again.

We stay like that for a few minutes, making out with my cock buried deep inside him.

"Need you to move," Dante pleads after a bit.

"Tell me if it hurts."

He nods, a soft smile on his lips. I move away to stand upright again before I thrust into him.

"Yes," Dante cries as I pick up speed. "So fucking good. Need... more," he pants out.

His cries of pleasure fill the room, and I can't deny his wishes, so I fuck him how we both love.

Hard and fast.

I allow myself to get lost in the moment, pounding into the man who stole my heart.

Grunts, moans, and the smacking of skin on skin are the soundtrack to our night as we both chase the high we desperately desire.

Dante's cock bobs against his stomach as I shift my hips to get a different angle. The head of his dick is leaking like a hose. I wrap my hand around him, using his precum as a natural lubricant to jack him off.

"I'm so close," Dante whimpers.

"Come for me, Treasure," I demand, thrusting into him even harder.

A tingle runs up the base of my spine as I run my fist up and down his hard length quickly.

"Fuck," he yells as warm liquid shoots out of him, a few drops hitting me in the face.

His channel squeezes tightly around me, and his orgasm takes over, pulling my own climax from me. I grunt and push into him farther, spilling my load deep in his ass before collapsing on top of him, bracing as much of my weight on my forearms as possible.

"That was amazing," Dante murmurs, running his fingers up and down my spine.

"So good" is all I can say, but it makes him laugh.

"I thought I was the one who was supposed to be fucked stupid," Dante teases.

"Whatever," I grumble, pulling out and standing up. "Let's clean up," I suggest with a tilt of my head and an outstretched hand.

Dante accepts, and when I pull him up, I wrap my arms around him and kiss him gently. "You're my everything, Treasure. I love you so fucking much."

He smiles against my lips. "Same."

I can't help but laugh as I pull him toward the bathroom.

"Brat."

Chapter 30

Dante

ANNA SLAPS MY HAND as I straighten the table's centerpiece in our backyard for the hundredth time. "Stop it," she yells.

"I just want it to be perfect," I grumble.

"It *is* perfect... but if you don't get your nerves under control, I'm pretty sure I'm going to have to get Mel to sedate you. I've never seen you this crazy before." I shrug.

Nixon is letting our guests in, and the box in my pocket is itching for me to touch it, but I fidget with my fingers instead.

Anna is the only one who knows I'm going to propose tonight, and that's only because I'm nervous as hell and acting like a damn fool.

"What if he says no?" I whisper.

Anna sighs. "Stop being an idiot. That man is *crazy* about you. He's going to say yes. Now take a deep breath." I do as she instructs. "Let it out." Slowly, I blow it out. "And relax." I try, but it's fucking hard.

Soon, everyone is making their way to the backyard. Hugs are shared, along with well-wishes on our trip. I try to smile and act normal, but Nixon keeps shooting me worried glances.

Maybe I shouldn't be an actor anymore. I clearly suck at it.

"Can I speak with you?" Nixon asks me.

I decide to say fuck it and propose now.

"After I ask you an important question."

Nixon's left brow raises, nodding for me to continue.

"Nixon, I love you. I want to spend my forever with you. You're it for me, babe. Will you marry me?" I pull out the ring box and drop to one knee.

Nixon doesn't respond right away, and he slowly shakes his head. I drop the box as my heart races.

"Are you okay?" he checks, dropping to his knees in front of me, concern lacing his tone.

"Why would I be okay?" I whimper. "You're saying no."

Nixon blows out a breath. "I'm not saying no. I was shaking my head because I was going to propose to *you*, silly."

Reaching into his back pocket, he pulls out a ring, and I can't help but laugh. Overcome with relief and joy, I launch myself into his arms.

"I'm taking that as a yes." He chuckles.

"As long as your answer is the same."

"You bet, babe. It's you and me for life," he whispers before kissing me, and all friends and family cheer.

"Please tell me this means you're going to be giving me grandbabies soon," Nixon's mom requests, rushing over to us and pulling us in for tight hugs.

"Maybe after Brazil," I reply, giving Nixon a knowing look.

We've been talking about kids a lot and would love to start a family soon, but it's also fun to give Mom a hard time, so we won't be telling her all the details yet. She doesn't need to know that Anna offered to be our surrogate quite yet. We'll keep that detail in our back pocket until it's closer to happening.

I can't believe how perfect my life is right now.

Who knew all it would take was for my life to get completely turned upside down and the hottest bodyguard in the world to come in and be my knight in shining armor?

The road wasn't smooth sailing for us, and we may face more twists and turns, but I know we'll get through them together.

Nixon was meant for me, and for better or worse, I'm never letting him go.

Epilogue

Nixon

Seven Months Later

Dante squeezes my hand as we sit in the courthouse, watching his father being handcuffed and taken away.

"I can't believe he's actually going to prison," he whispers.

The trial for Arnold Michaelson lasted a few weeks longer than we would have liked, but the jury made the right decision. As a result, we won't have to worry about him anymore.

"Some people know the difference between right and wrong," I remind him, squeezing his hand.

The second we get home, Anna runs toward us, launching herself into Dante's arms.

"Congratulations," she shouts, and Dante spins her around.

Brittany laughs as she walks over to us and stands beside me.

"I'm just glad he actually has to face his consequences for once," Dante replies as he holds his best friend.

We know he won't have as long of a sentence as a normal person would, but it doesn't matter. What matters is he lost, and we won.

"I have other good news," Anna tells him, stepping back.

Her face is lit up as she stares at us, and I wonder why she's so excited. I look at Brittany, who is also smiling brightly, and when I raise my brow at her, she shakes her head and tilts it toward Anna, telling me to wait and listen.

"Spit it out," Dante grumbles, clearly frustrated with her delay.

Anna rolls her eyes, walks to the counter, and grabs a Ziploc baggie with a pregnancy test inside.

My heart freezes when I realize what's happening.

"Are you serious?" I ask, but the words come out a little rough since my throat is thick with emotions.

She nods with the biggest grin. "I'm pregnant. Congratulations. You're going to be fathers," she yells.

Dante collapses to the floor, tears running down his face. "It's really happening?" He gasps for air as he looks up at his best friend.

Anna blinks quickly as her own tears bubble to the surface.

"It is," she whispers as she kneels and pulls Dante into her arms.

I join them on the floor in a group hug, with Brittany following my move, and we all sit and cry, embracing this moment.

Dante and I have cried a lot in our time together, but these aren't tears of sadness, pain, or grief. They're tears of joy. Our lives are actually moving in the direction we've been planning, and I couldn't be happier.

Not only do I have the man of my dreams, but we're going to be fathers. And his best friend is our surrogate. Our world is only going to get better from here.

When I took on Dante as a client, I wasn't planning on finding the man I'd spend the rest of my life with, but I did, and I'll thank the universe every day that I get to keep him.

Thank you so much for reading Nixon! I hope you enjoyed it. If you did I would love for you to leave a positive review!

Looking for more bodyguard love? Denver is up next! Pre-Order Denver: an m/m best friends to lovers, bodyguard romance now!

Acknowledgements

THANK YOU SO MUCH for reading Nixon! I had so much fun writing this book!

As always there is so many people to thank, because it takes a village to write a book.

First I want to thank my amazing team. Without them I would be an absolute mess! Brittany Franks and Suzanne Talkington are the real MVPs! They hold me together when I want to fall apart and mean the world to me!

Secondly I want to thank my superb Alpha/Beta Readers Mandy, Meaghan, and Robin. These ladies are always pointing out the beginning issues and are always available for me to bounce ideas off of. I'd probably still be stuck trying to figure things out if it wasn't for them.

My sensitivity reader JP Jackson. I don't think I would feel comfortable writing an m/m romance without his input. He makes me a better author and I love our conversations so much. I am so lucky to have found JP and to be able to call him a friend.

My editing team who helped me polish this book and make it as strong as it is today! Chantell, Nay, Kaylene and Nikki at Swish Designs and Editing were so amazing to work with as always! They really helped me strength this book and make it what it is today!

My cover designer for creating the **perfect** cover for this book! Brittany with Chaotic Creatives knocked it out of the park and I mean it when I say I drooled a little when she sent me this cover!

My amazingly hilarious friend Mikayla Christy for helping me write the "Duck not dick" scene. I was complaining about how Word kept wanting me to change dick to duck which led to a funny conversation which birthed the scene that made me laugh out loud.

My family for putting up with me when I put myself on a deadline and go a little crazy.

And last but obviously not least... you.. the reader... without you I wouldn't be continuing to put books out! Thank you for your continued support. I love you all so much!

There are a lot more books of mine coming soon so make sure to sign up for my newsletter to stay up to date on everything I have up my sleeve!

Also by Laura John

6. Clean Slates (A fast burn rock star romance)

7. Tangled Love (A rock star romance love triangle romance)

8. Restless Beat (A rock star romance)

9. Love In Sienna Boxset (Books 1-4)

10. Love in Sienna Boxset (Books 5-8)

Sentinel Protection Duology

1. Fighting Attraction (A M/M bodyguard romance)

2. Embracing Temptation (A M/M age gap bodyguard romance)

Standalones

1. Monster In The Shadows (Dark romance standalone)

2. Kissing in the snow (A M/M Christmas Novella set in the Sentinel Protection World)

3. Afterglow (A kinky brother's best friend romance)

About Author

LAURA IS A STEAMY romance author from Alberta, Canada, who melds love and angst together while normalizing mental illness. She also brings a mixture of m/m and m/f books because love is love. In her books, you will fall in love with her rock stars, bodyguards, baseball players, a small town and even a hired hit man!

When she's not writing, Laura enjoys reading, going to concerts, hiking, and experimenting with makeup!